COWBOY
LUST

COWBOY LUST

EROTIC ROMANCE
FOR WOMEN

Edited by
Delilah Devlin

Foreword by
Lorelei James

Published in the United States by Cleis Press, Inc., 2246 Sixth Street, Berkeley, California 94710.

Printed in the United States.
Cover design: Scott Idleman/Blink
Cover photograph: Lonnie Duka/Getty Images
Text design: Frank Wiedemann
First Edition.
10 9 8 7 6 5 4 3 2 1

Trade paper ISBN: 978-1-57344-814-7
E-book ISBN: 978-1-57344-828-4

Contents

FOREWORD

I ♥ cowboys. I always have; I always will.

When I was asked to write this foreword for an anthology devoted to hot cowboy tales, I yelled, "*Yee-haw*!" Then I wondered how I'd only limit myself to a couple of paragraphs. It'd take so much more, a whole book (or thirty!) to explain how much I love writing about these rough and tumble guys who often appear larger than life—even when those same strong, capable men I admire so greatly would smoothly change the subject when being called iconic, because that humbleness is also part of who they are.

One question I get asked frequently is: *why do you write about cowboys?* Is it because I've been surrounded by cowboy culture since I was knee high to a grasshopper? Yes. Every day I'm grateful that I grew up in the western United States, where being a real cowboy isn't just an attitude or a slogan on a T-shirt, but a way of life. Yet...there are different types of cowboys and each one holds a special charm. And what a fulfilling job it is, getting to spread that cowboy love and adding in those components of sexy naughtiness that makes a cowboy the ultimate man and the quintessential alpha hero.

It's no surprise that cowboys have held the interest of readers for many years. In traditional western fiction, the cowboy is the embodiment of all that is good, honest, and true. Not only is the cowboy the guy you'd want at your side or watching your back during a gunfight, or a bar fight, but he's the stand-up guy other men look up to and ladies moon over. A cowboy's values are at the core of who he is. His love of land drives him day in, day out to provide for his family. And *whoo-ee*—there is something mighty compelling about a man who works with his hands and loves getting down and dirty. So much of who a cowboy is comes from what he does: caring for livestock, being a steward and student of the land, whether that land is in Wyoming, Texas, Hawaii, or someplace in between.

And yet, there is loneliness that comes with living in rural America, whether it was one hundred fifty years ago, or right now. Whether we're talking about a rancher cowboy or those cowboys that put in many miles, alone, on the long stretches of back roads and highways.

Rodeo cowboys are the risk takers locked in that age-old battle of man versus beast. It's more than showmanship—seeing those guys roughed up, dirty, and determined is the epitome of hard-edged sexiness. It's a show of sheer grit when a bull rider climbs on the back of a fifteen-hundred-pound animal. It's a test of wills as a saddle bronc or bareback rider tries to hang on for eight seconds as a buckin' horse attempts to throw him in the dirt. Doesn't it make you want to strip him naked, find his bumps, bruises, scrapes, and scars and kiss them all better? Those team ropers invoke many female fantasies of being double-teamed and thoroughly trussed up. Talk about power and guts—watch a bull dogger launch himself off a horse at a full gallop to bring a steer to the ground. These rodeo cowboys know how to perform and ride hard—on and off the dirt.

I'll admit a cowboy's physical attributes play a large role in the timeless appeal of these rugged men. Because, come on...is there *anything* sexier than a guy wearing boots, jeans, and a hat? Hearing the jingle jangle of spurs and the soft flap of a pair of leather chaps as he saunters toward you. Seeing a face shadowed beneath that cowboy hat—and then the dusty brim slowly lifting up to reveal a handsome face and a devilish grin. *Swoon.* Then there are those acres of muscles, earned the hard way from hours of physical labor, muscles that ripple beneath a crisply pressed western shirt. It's mesmerizing, watching how a cowboy's body moves as one with his horse as he's working cattle or just riding the range. And isn't that the definitive fantasy? Experiencing how well that hard toned masculine body moves between the sheets and the single-minded focus that carries from the barnyard and rodeo arena into the bedroom.

So when taking the elements of a traditional western and adding in erotic romance, you get the best of both worlds—a smokin' hot, take charge cowboy who gets the girl in the end, rather than riding off into the sunset alone. It's gratifying in erotic western romance to finally kick that bedroom door wide open and see just what the heck makes that man tick. To get a front row seat to his hidden passion, his sexual inventiveness, and to witness the sweetness that a tough man will show only to the woman who owns him, heart and soul. Because cowboys are a breed apart, it takes a special lady to see beneath that gruff exterior. A woman willing to unlock that passionate side, any time, anywhere—against the barn, or in a dusty pickup, over a hay bale, or in a soft bed at the end of a long day. A woman that knows actions speak louder than words. A woman who understands that once you've had a cowboy's boots under your bed and a big, strong body keeping you hot every night, you'll never settle for anything less.

Feeling that tingle of lust yet? Luckily, there are several great short stories in store for you to kick that lust into high gear. Can I get a *yee-haw*?

My hat is off to all the great contributors to *Cowboy Lust*! Readers are in for a real treat—so sit back, prop your boots up on the coffee table, and enjoy the ride.

Long live cowboys!

Lorelei James
The New York Times and *USA Today* bestselling author of the Rough Riders series and the Blacktop Cowboys® series

INTRODUCTION

There's a reason Western romance stories never go out of fashion. The cowboy is an iconic figure that embodies the dichotomy of the fiercely independent, earthy alpha male while being a nurturing protector. Given a picture of a man on a horse, wearing Wranglers and chaps, with a broad-rimmed hat shadowing his face, women melt. *I* melt. Admittedly, I'm a pretty jaded reader, but I still crave the romantic idea of that gruff, capable man.

Even when he's up to his knees in mud freeing a calf from a wallow, his image doesn't tarnish. The imagination sparks, filling in the details—the scent of horse, cow, and crisp, clean sweat; the sight of sun-leathered skin and crow's feet; the feel of work-hardened thighs and arms; the sound of a deep-voiced Texas drawl.

Maybe my abiding affection for Western romances is grounded in the nine years I lived in the heart of the Texas Hill Country with a working ranch nestled up against my backyard fence. Cowboys wearing Wranglers, straw hats, and boots were a common sight. The slower pace of life there was a soothing balm after life in a corporate cubicle. The romance of the place—despite the dust, tarantulas, scorpions, and snakes—enthralled me. Still does.

So when I put out the word that I was looking for "cowboy" stories, I had high expectations. The writers delivered!

From Cari Quinn's "Riding Double," which has a wicked twist, to the final story, Anna Meadows's haunting "She Don't Stay the Night," you'll travel a breathtaking sweep of distinct voices, settings, and themes.

Veteran erotica writer Cheyenne Blue will take you to the Australian outback in "Under the Southern Cross" for a riveting tale with a heroine on the run for her life. In "Drought," Michael Bracken tells a quieter, simpler tale of a cowboy and a school-teacher that's no less compelling.

If that's not enough, you'll find a female rodeo star determined to win back her buckle and her confidence in M. Marie's "Rough Stock," a gun-toting girlfriend set on firing up the hussy who laid hands on her man in Lissa Matthews's "Small-Town Famous," and a gunslinging couple seeking revenge in the Wild West in Chaparrita's "Raney's Last Ride."

Bored yet? I dare you to give this collection a try. You'll find humor, heart-melting romance, and sweet—as well as rough—lovin' in these here pages. *Saddle up, y'all!*

Delilah Devilin

RIDING DOUBLE

Cari Quinn

Y ou're really willing to let me at your man?"

Danica Connor stopped chopping celery and set aside her knife. "Col, he's not my man. We haven't slept together." *Yet*. There was a serious *yet* implied there, at least if Jack got his way. "Besides, I was thinking of a one-night stand. Just a way for you to burn off some steam. To remember you're still a woman under the pinstripes."

Perched atop the center island, Colleen glanced down at her attire and grinned. "No pinstripes here."

Danica eyed her sister and grinned back. No, she definitely didn't look like a budding economics professor in that getup. Cut-off denim shorts hugged shapely tanned thighs, and two pink triangles connected by string barely covered nature's bounty up top. Twin honey-blonde ponytails draped over her shoulders.

Danica glanced down at her own outfit—ratty overalls and a T-shirt with a hole under the armpit. Even though they looked exactly alike, Col had the sexy all sewn up. "Which proves my point. This would be a great time to go see Jack."

Danica reached up to undo her hair from its tightly coiled bun. She'd been mucking horse stalls all afternoon, and she figured she smelled like straw and mud and things even worse. A long hot shower would cure most of her ills, minus the annoying buzz of awareness she felt between her thighs every time her friendly neighbor, Jack Benton, came over to help her deal with her new farm. Jack always offered his assistance, and she usually gave him a glass of ice-cold lemonade and a healthy dose of flirting for his trouble.

Tonight, she had a hankering to give him something else entirely.

"Why would you want to share him with me?"

"Whoa, whoa. Share him?" Danica tossed aside a piece of straw that had gotten embedded in her hair. "How can I share something that isn't mine?"

Colleen clearly had a different definition of her relationship with Jack than she did. They were only flirting and getting to know each other.

Just spending hours together week after week after week, riding horses, taking care of the animals, working the land. Occasionally holding hands and engaging in brief, smoking kisses that tasted even better because she never let them go too far.

Nothing like self-denial to fan the flames of desire—or damn-near forest fire of desire, judging by last night's lip lock and tongue tangle.

"All I know is I've been here two days and whenever he comes around, you start blushing and giggling like a high school girl. You barely introduced me before you asked me to go shovel shit." Colleen reached for a stray stalk of celery Danica had yet to butcher. "Now you're saying you're up for me diddling him. What's wrong with this picture?"

Danica reached for the plastic bowl of chicken salad she was putting together for dinner. One amazing thing about moving home and taking over her deceased parents' ranch had been getting used to eating real food again, instead of the overprocessed crap she'd scarfed down every night after long photo shoots back in the city.

After their father's unexpected death, she'd come home to evaluate her options: either tackle the ranch—a small one by the standards of Laurel Creek, Colorado, but still pretty big to a born-again city girl—or put it up for sale. Colleen's divorce had made her think that they could handle things together, but Colleen wasn't interested in working the land. She hadn't stayed for more than a few weeks before returning home to Nevada for summer classes. Now that it was almost fall, Colleen had come up for a quick weekend visit.

A couple of months ago she would've felt resentful about Colleen's lack of help, but she'd found the rhythm to rural life and no longer felt as if she was drowning. With the help of a few local boys and Jack, she'd actually been managing pretty well.

So well, in fact, that she'd made arrangements to take a photography job in Chicago for the month of October. A whole month. If things went well back here at the ranch under the care of the young men she'd entrusted the place to, she could take more such jobs.

That was her life. Her *real* life, not one of boring domesticity with Jack. Not squeezing out babies and whipping up pies and rocking her ass off on the glider he'd built for her himself. He hadn't asked for any of that, of course, but he had "happy home-maker" tattooed in invisible ink on his bronzed shoulders.

"I didn't say I was up for you sleeping with him alone. What

I suggested is that we have a little fun tonight before you head home to Vegas." Danica dumped the celery into the chicken salad and cocked an eyebrow at her sister. "You remember high school, right?"

To Danica's shock, Colleen flushed. "That was years ago."

"We're only twenty-six," Danica reminded her, wondering if maybe Colleen was right.

She hadn't even considered taking another walk on the wild side until this afternoon. Jack had come by with a gift of moonstone earrings he'd "picked up" for her from a craft fair in town, and then he'd asked her to dinner at Laurel Creek's one and only fancy restaurant next Friday night.

Almost a whole week away. As if he were courting her.

She liked Jack. A lot. Too much, probably, since if her October photography trip went well, she'd be going out on similar work jaunts every few months. She wasn't long-term material. She didn't even want to be. After being shackled too young and for too long—and for what?—she wanted her freedom. Best for Jack if he understood up front what she was looking for.

Sex? Sure. Flirting, conversation, taking in a movie. But the roots she'd come back here to tend didn't include settling down with a man. Not yet. Maybe not ever.

"Yeah, but I'm divorced now," Colleen said. "And you're... well, you and Steve—"

"Divorced means single. Right?" She waited for Colleen's reluctant nod. "And Steve's newly married, which makes him not my problem. So why don't we just go for it?" She cursed as she scraped the side of her thumb on the sharp underside of the bowl's rim. "Just fun, Col. A couple of orgasms. Then you'll go home tomorrow and I'll..."

"What?" Colleen questioned, crunching into her celery.

"Enjoy my life," Danica finished, grabbing a fork to sample

her chicken salad. She took a bite and then reached for the small bowl of chopped bacon she'd set aside. After dumping it in, she tried the salad again.

Yep, still true. Everything was better with bacon.

"Making chicken salad and knitting," Colleen's smirk widened as Danica reached out to smack her sister's thigh, "in between your country threesomes."

"Your call. You don't want to go there, I understand. And it's not like Jack knows what I have in mind."

"Yeah, what about Jack? How do you know he won't slam the door in your face?"

Danica stirred her salad one last time and grabbed the box of clear wrap. "Hmm. A pair of tanned blond twins wearing next to nothing show up at his ranch to offer him a full-body massage. What do *you* think he'll do?"

Colleen sighed. "I thought *I* was the bad twin."

"This isn't bad. This is about showing how good we can be." Danica grinned. "It's actually a neighborly service we're providing, if you think of it right."

Best of all, Jack would know she wasn't interested in anything heavy if she didn't mind him having sex with her sister. That would send a crystal clear message, now, wouldn't it? Plus Colleen might stop looking so mopey if she did something sorta crazy. Since her divorce, her life had been about work and school. *Only* work and school.

They all needed a wild night. She sure as hell did. Especially if it meant that Jack would finally get the hint and stop bringing her carnations like she was his junior high crush.

"You're crazy, Dani."

"You know you love it. So what's your answer? In or out?"

Colleen shook her head, smiling. "We're not sixteen anymore."

"Thank God. But we can still give this cowboy a ride he'll never forget." Danica tapped her fork against her lips. "C'mon. He's fucking hot."

"Yeah." Colleen sighed and twirled a lock of her hair. Danica knew she was imagining Jack's chocolate brown eyes and his loose, blond-tipped brown hair. Long but not too long—just enough to give a woman a good handful. And his body? All those muscles and tanned skin, finished off with a princely bulge just south of the Benton Ranch crest on his shiny gold belt buckle.

"He never wears a shirt," Colleen said, her tone dreamy.

"I don't think he owns any. Good thing, since that barrel of a chest qualifies as the eighth wonder of the world." At Col's laugh, Danica lifted her brows. "So? You in?"

A light of challenge kindled in Colleen's eyes as she jumped down from the counter. "All right, sis. You're on."

Jack Benton looked up from the saddle he was shining when he heard the crunch of gravel. He saw his arrivals but noticed the sky behind them first, only because it was a lot darker than it had been just a few moments before. The dark, threatening clouds cast a pall over the Sangre de Cristo Mountains, making them appear foreboding rather than welcoming. A tangle of tumbleweeds blew past him just before the rising wind made its presence known with a howl.

Storm's moving in.

Noting the twin blondes marching toward him, he suspected it would be storming on more than one front. His quick inhalation brought with it the scent of rain. So that made two things he could expect: an imminent downpour and, if his tightening Levis were any indication, instant and irreversible cock strangulation.

What the hell were they doing here?

Danica and Colleen Yardley were knockouts on their own. But together? Strutting down the drive in similar summer outfits, long blonde hair flying behind them, pouty pink lips tilting in matching come-hither smiles... Dear God. In a second he'd need to lower his zipper to keep from popping the teeth.

"Evenin', ladies." Jack tipped his hat to them and shifted his body closer to the saddle. If they saw the wood he was sporting, they might get the wrong idea. Then again, those deviously sexy smiles suggested they were offering a lot more than the last woman who'd stopped by hawking magazine subscriptions. "What brings you out this way?"

"Just out for a stroll. And since your ranch is the only one within miles, this seemed like a place to stop and wait out the storm." Danica's voice had an extra added purr to it, which didn't help the tightness in his crotch. She walked forward and set her petal-pink fingertips on the edge of the saddle stand. "Don't s'pose you'd let us stay here for a while? Just to be safe."

Jack lifted his face to the wind and took another breath. Ozone stung his nostrils. "We have a few minutes. More than enough time for you to head home."

"Well, now, that's not very gentlemanly." Colleen stepped closer and ran a predatory hand over his damp chest. The sun had been out in full force all day, and he'd only climbed down from Silba a little while ago. He probably stunk of sweat, but Colleen sure didn't seem to mind. Strange, considering she'd been nothing more than polite both times he'd met her this weekend.

He cocked a brow and looked from one woman to the other. Did they really think they had him snowed? He knew which of them was which without any trouble. Months of working alongside a woman, you got to know her little tics. The way she nervously shoved her hair behind her ear, how her eyes would get all squinty when she was trying to think of something to say. Whatever game these two were playing, he still knew exactly which woman leaned up to lay her soft wet lips on his.

Colleen could kiss, all right, but she wasn't Dani. *His* Dani, whether or not she cared to recognize that fact. He could wait her out.

"Maybe we can change your mind about sending us home." Danica moved against his side. She cupped his erection and lifted her face to his. "Sure you won't let us come...inside?"

A dead man would've responded to the double entendre in her question. A smart man would've said "Hell yes!" and led the way up to his king-sized bed. But Jack Benton wasn't dead, and he'd never been called smart, so he picked option three and finally asked the question he'd been tempted to ask since they arrived.

"What the hell are you up to?"

Danica blinked, her eyelashes already dewy from the soft rain now beginning to fall. "Huh?"

"You heard me." As thunder forked in the rolling, steel-gray sky, he gripped the twins' forearms and led them toward the back porch. They had a good amount of ground to cover, but between his no-nonsense grip and the pelting rain, the women kept up fine. He yanked open the rickety screen door and stood back, motioning them inside. "Sit down while I grab the saddle," he said.

When he returned, the two of them sat at the table with sheepish expressions on their faces. Their dripping wet clothes clung to them. Colleen wore a bikini top, but Danica had on a tight tank top with no bra, revealing her nipples in sharp detail. His dick rallied again, but he shut the back door and willed his brain to work.

He tossed his hat down on the table. "So which of you's gonna get to explaining?"

"Explain what?" Danica's innocent look almost made him grin. Almost.

"Why you both sashayed up my drive looking for trouble."

"Did we find it?" Danica asked, batting her lashes. He'd never seen her bat her lashes nor do anything artificial. She was all woman, no girl, and he wondered about this change—even as his body responded to it.

But that didn't mean he'd just go along with this setup. He didn't appreciate them thinking he functioned only with his dick. Other parts of him engaged too, now and then. Which they were about to find out.

"A gentleman never turns down a willing lady," he said, striding to Colleen and gripping her arm. "Come on, sweet thing."

"Wait!" Danica protested as Colleen's bluebell eyes rounded. "This party's supposed to be for three."

"Is it now? I'm not into threesomes." He glanced at Colleen. "My bedroom's just down the hall."

"Um, okay." Colleen tossed Danica a quick glance and rose, her breasts brushing Jack's chest on the way up. "But Dani—"

"Can listen," he said, tugging Colleen along behind him.

Once they were in his spacious bedroom, he flipped on the lights. Rain slashed against the windows, insulating them. A good thing if she'd been Dani, a bad thing for what he had in mind.

He tipped Colleen's face closer to his. "Spill it. What's going on?"

Nervously, she wet her lips. "It was Dani's idea."

"I figured that." He loosened his hold on her chin and gently rubbed his thumb over the lower lip she'd bitten until it was

swollen. "Wanna have some fun with your sister?" At her horrified look, he chuckled. "Not that kind of fun. Just follow my
lead."

Before she could argue, he dipped his head toward hers.

Danica folded her hands together and swallowed over her rising
aggravation. As pissed as she was, she could actually taste it. A
sharp moan rang out, carrying all the way down the damn hall,
and she leapt to her feet.

What the hell? Was he attacking her sister or what?

She rubbed her forehead. *Calm down.* Hardly attacking.
And this had been her bright idea. She just hadn't expected Jack
to want Colleen more than her. For fuck's sake, they looked
alike. How could he be more attracted to Colleen? Especially
since he hadn't shown Colleen one bit of interest beyond friend-
ship before this very moment.

Another rippling moan floated out to her over the insistent
rain. That was it. She'd had *e*-fucking-*nough*.

She marched down the hall. If Colleen was naked in Jack's
bed, it wouldn't be for long.

This had been the worst idea ever. What kind of man wasn't
into threesomes? Wasn't that a biological imperative, like caring
about football or drinking orange juice out of the carton?

Whatever. He wasn't getting twosome sex tonight, either.
She pressed a hand on his partially open bedroom door and
sucked in a breath, bracing herself for the worst. Maybe they
were already having sex. Jack seemed like a guy who moved
fast.

She stepped inside the doorway and stopped, her anger
building even before her eyes set upon them. Then she blinked.
They were sitting on the bed. Fully dressed. Not kissing or
even groping each other. Colleen's hair was barely mussed. Her

lipstick, however, had smeared a smidgen.

Even that made Danica's skin prickle with irritation. "What's going on here?"

"What's it look like, darlin'?" Jack cupped Colleen's shoulder, drawing more of Danica's ire with just the movement of his fingers.

"I heard moans."

Colleen shrugged and patted his taut stomach. His *bare* stomach. "Sometimes a girl's just gotta release some stress."

"Yeah, I hear you there." Danica crossed her arms over her chest. "Mind leaving us alone, Col?"

"Not at all." Colleen touched Jack's jean-clad thigh, and Danica's pulse beat a nasty tattoo in her temple. "Good luck, cowboy."

"Shut the door behind you, will you?" Jack asked.

Colleen smiled. "Sure thing." A moment later they were alone.

It wasn't his fault. She knew that. She'd set up this whole dumb scenario. Her inability to foresee exactly how much she'd hate to watch Jack touching her sister—or vice versa—was to blame, not Jack.

"So what's this about?" he asked softly. "You tryin' to push me away, Dani?"

"I thought it would be fun. That *all* of us could have fun. But it wasn't. What kind of guy doesn't like threesomes?" she demanded as he rose and walked over to her.

"A guy who's already set his sights on the woman he wants. Singular." He coiled a lock of her hair around his finger and a zing of heat traveled straight up to her scalp. "Got a problem with that?"

"Maybe." She moved closer, rubbing her breasts against his chest while she risked a glance into his eyes. The intensity in them scared her, especially since she felt an answering echo in her chest. "I'm not a settling down kind of woman, Jack. It's not fair to you to pretend otherwise."

A half-smile tipped up his smug mouth. "Who said anything about settling? I just want us to enjoy each other."

He gripped her hips and boosted her up, giving her little choice but to wrap her legs around his butt. Not that she wanted to resist. Then he crushed his mouth to hers. *Mmm.* She could taste the whiskey he'd drunk earlier. She sucked eagerly on his flesh, sinking deeper into the kiss. Into *him.*

All at once, thoughts of her sister receded. At least until he jiggled her in his arms and slipped his deliciously rough palm under her tank.

She drew back and gasped. "What about Colleen?"

"She understands. And she's got the keys to my truck." He gave her a sexy smile that sent flutters through her stomach and pulled her nipples to tight peaks. With a few tugs of his fingers, he yanked up her shirt and exposed her breasts. He let out a low growl. "Look at all that pretty skin you've been hiding from me."

Though she laughed, she arched up, yearning for him so much it shocked her. She didn't want to worry about expectations now. He was right. Enjoyment was so much more uncomplicated. "I wanted to go slow."

"Until you wanted to go fast."

He quirked a brow at her, and she laughed again. God, he made her happy. Giddy, even. Her laughter turned to giggles when he dumped her on the bed. She bounced on the firm mattress and grabbed the sheets as he dipped his talented mouth to her breast.

"Well, don't let it be said I don't know how to oblige a lady," he said, nipping at her beaded tip while he undid his belt.

With just those words, she started to throb. She leaned up to push more of her nipple between his teeth and clutched at his hair to hold him where he was. As far as she was concerned, he could stay there forever.

Too soon he moved his attention to her torso, then lower as he drew off her shorts. Another growl left his throat as he saw she wasn't wearing panties. He fastened his lips to her swollen pussy, and then she was the one growling, begging, tugging on his hair to bring his tongue inside her. Faster, deeper. He nuzzled her clit and rubbed his nose over the narrow thatch of curls, but he didn't pleasure her like she wanted.

The jerk didn't want her to come yet. That much was clear from his glistening smile as he drew his used mouth away and removed his jeans and boxers.

"Fast, remember?" His rasp only excited her more as he withdrew a condom from the nightstand and drew the pointed end of the packet across her oversensitized nipple. She shivered and he grinned. "If you think you can take it."

"Oh, I'll take it," she gritted out. But she doubted her threshold when she took a good look at his thick length. That shiny crest on his belt had distracted her from Jack's natural gifts. His hard, golden flesh made her mouth water. "*Now.*"

He suited up and notched his cock at her soaked entrance, barely slipping inside. He drew her legs up over his elbows and rocked, his glittering brown eyes holding her captive as he rocked shallowly into her again and again.

"Damn it, Jack. Never took you for a fucking tease."

"You haven't taken me at all yet." He grinned again and coasted home, gliding deep in one smooth thrust. "Now you have."

Unless an unintelligible grunt counted as an answer, she didn't reply. She spread her legs wide and clasped her own nipples, rolling them between her fingers while the music of their lovemaking played through her mind. The slap of flesh, Jack's grunts, her helpless moans.

It went too quickly. Even expecting the climax, she couldn't prepare for it, because his steady surges inside her welcoming body hit her in all the right ways. The orgasm gripped her like the storm outside rocked the house, shaking her foundation and blanketing her in warmth at the same time.

"You hid that from me," he whispered, flicking his thumb over her clit. She trembled as if he'd smacked her. "I like watching you come." He pushed deeper and added a hip swivel that made whorls of color explode behind her closed lids. "Like feeling it, too."

She clenched around him, flexing her hips until he couldn't talk anymore. His ragged breath rang in her ears, blowing sweet over her skin as his body jerked and she felt the hot pulse of his release into the condom.

Then he sprawled on top of her, pinning her to the mattress with the delicious weight of his warm, damp body. The storm still raged outside, but in this bed she was as satisfied and as comfortable as she'd ever been.

Not that she could claim to be dry. *That* was one statement she'd never be able to make around Jack Benton.

"You're so pretty," he said, parting the tangle of her hair to trail kisses down the side of her face. "I'm probably crushing you."

"A little," she admitted.

He pulled out of her, and she sighed at the loss of his heat. He smiled and disposed of the condom before gathering her in his arms again. "Better?"

"Best," she murmured, snuggling against his chest. She loved the sound of his pounding heart, knowing she'd caused it to beat faster. The salty perspiration on his skin tasted so good when she licked his nipple that she did it again, stopping only when he groaned.

"Tell me this wasn't a one-time thing, Dani. Please."

The unexpected emotion in his voice made her lift her head. Her throat closed as she glimpsed the need in his eyes. "Jack, I'm a photographer. I go out on jobs. I took one in October, in Chicago."

"How long will you be gone?"

That was it? No demands for her to stay, no complaints? Her ex never would've accepted her decision to go away that easily. In fact, Steve had never accepted it, which was one reason he was now her ex.

But Steve and Jack were as far apart as two men could get. Comparing them wasn't only unfair, it didn't even make sense.

"Just a month. This time. Sometimes they're longer jobs. In farther-flung places."

He nodded and wound her hair around his wrist. "You're so talented. I want a copy of that seascape hanging over your couch for over there." He nodded to the bare wall opposite them. "I've been saving that spot."

She couldn't have stopped her smile if she'd tried. "You really like my work?"

"I love it." He hugged her close and brushed a kiss over her hair. "I don't want to take over your life, Dani. Just share whatever pieces you'll give me."

Impossibly moved, she laid her hand over his heart and reveled in the strong, steady beat. Here was the anchor she hadn't realized she'd been looking for, the safe place she could return to no matter how far away she traveled. A haven where she could always be herself, with a man she was learning to trust.

"I'm good at sharing," she whispered. "If you'll give me time,

I'll get even better."

"I'll give you all the time you need. In the meantime, how about I show you how good *I* am at certain things?"

With a grin, he dove down her body and set to work proving his point.

UNDER THE SOUTHERN CROSS

Cheyenne Blue

No city lights here." The glowing tip of Jake's cigarette pierced the gathering darkness. "No convenience stores as you Americans need, either."

"No," I agreed.

He scowled at me from under his wide-brimmed Akubra hat. "Just a load of bloody sheep and spinifex that'll pierce the sole of your boot." He took a deep drag on the cigarette. "An outback sheep station isn't on most people's ten-day tour of Australia."

"It's not," I agreed again. I spread my legs for balance and tipped back my chair to sight the Southern Cross. Those five stars low on the southern horizon represented everything strange about this place.

"So what's a sheila like you doing here? You're a city girl."

Jake's persistence was annoying. A truthful answer was impossible, and I was too tired to invent a plausible lie. Agent Dolan had told me no one would ask questions. But Jake was a casual worker, a jackaroo, as I'd learned to call the Australian cowboys who came looking for work. The manager took him on for two weeks and told me to stay out of his way.

I've never been good at taking orders.

Jake flicked me a half-smile as he leaned on the verandah rail, an invitation I couldn't resist.

"I needed a change," I said, in an approximation of the truth.

He snorted. "Right. And I'm a cocky's missus." He pulled a beer from the cooler at his feet, offered it to me, and sat down. "We're not going anywhere this evening. Why don't you tell me your tale?"

For a second, I considered it. I've always been gullible if I think someone is taking an interest. Agent Dolan's words ran through my head: "Your safety depends on your discretion. The FBI can only do so much to protect you."

Malory Station in Western Australia was a reliable shelter for those under the witness protection program, and I wasn't going to blow my cover. Jake wouldn't believe me anyway. Instead of answering, I looked back at the sky. The Milky Way trailed across the heavens, brighter than in L.A. I imagined how far each star must have traveled in its lifetime, how separated they were from one another. Like me.

Suddenly, I felt very alone. My longing for L.A. overwhelmed me. This place was alien, surreal. Even the buzz of the insects, which had seemed so comforting before, made me uneasy.

"Nothing to tell." I glanced at him.

"Everyone has a story." His huge brown paw touched my thigh with surprising softness.

I studied it. Jake worked with his hands. I'd seen him earlier, thighs clamped around his stock horse like a nutcracker, those same hands working ropes, reins, and fencing posts.

His fingers moved on my skin, crawled higher. The grit of

the desert transferred from his fingers to my thigh. The friction seemed to spark a connection between us, fragile and tenuous now, but it was there, strung as taut as fencing wire.

I rested back against the chair where the wicker unraveled like the L.A. freeways and contemplated Jake. He wouldn't fit into my world; he would stick out like dog's balls in the L.A. bar scene. But here, he flowed seamlessly into the landscape. He wore the uniform of the outback male: a man's undershirt— they called it a singlet here—an Akubra hat, and a dusty pair of jeans.

"What brings you here?" I asked.

"Heard this place had a good foreman. One who lets us get on with it."

"Get on with what?"

"Mustering. Cutting and branding cattle, mending fences. No health and bloody safety lectures."

Jake's hand shifted higher on my thigh, but although I was definitely interested, I stood. If he was the only amusement here, I'd make him wait and sweat a bit. That would make it all the better when it happened.

"I'm going to bed." I pretended not to notice his half-smile as his hand fell away from my leg.

As I ambled off, Jake swung his feet onto the verandah railing, cigarette smoke curling lazily to the stars.

I didn't see Jake the next morning, but when I went out to the verandah after dinner, a tang of sweat and dust told me I wasn't alone.

"Still here?"

I saw his face in profile. The starlight etched his cheekbone into steel. "Where else would I go?"

"Someone was asking after you. I was on the radio to Avoca

Downs, and they said someone had driven up looking for an American."

I stared, nerves instantly jangling. No one just "drives up" to outback stations. "Who was it?"

"No idea. They said their cousin was jillarooing on a station, and they wanted to drop in."

I processed that information. "I don't have cousins."

"Guess they're wrong then."

I could hardly swallow for the crushing weight of fear in my throat. Until now, it had been a game, one I'd expected would follow the rules. I was to stay here until the case came to trial, at which point they'd recall me to Los Angeles to give evidence. Then they'd relocate me permanently to an anonymous large American city.

Americans looking for their cousin. Maybe it was really as simple as that. But the leaping waves of panic kept coming.

Jake was still staring at me. "You okay? You're looking crook as a dog all of a sudden."

I forced a laugh. "I'm fine. Just hoping it's not Uncle Bertie deciding to drop in."

"Even if he finds out where you are, he's still a day's drive away."

"Maybe I won't be here when he arrives."

"Where will you go?"

"I'll take a bedroll. Stay out overnight."

For long moments the only sound was the whirr of the insects.

"Must be serious, whatever you're running from." Cigarette smoke curled lazily through the air. "You've never shown any interest in going bush. I'm fencing near Bulloo Bore tomorrow—come along if you want. I'm camping, but you'll be safe with me."

I hoped he was right.

I didn't sleep well that night. Thoughts of Tatamura and what he would do kept looping through my head. Each loop had a worse ending than the one before. I'd seen too much when I'd walked innocently and unknowingly into the backroom of Tatamura's bar, just a contract cleaner wanting to do her job and go home. I'd seen the piles of banknotes, the bags of white powder, and the spread-eagled body of a man pegged out on the floor. How could a man suffer so much pain and still be alive...

The FBI said my evidence would put Tatamura away for thirty years. And if he went down, one of the biggest drug cartels in the L.A. Basin would collapse.

When I woke before dawn, my skin filmy with sweat, I gave up trying to sleep. I threw clothes into a bag and stole down to the kitchen to put coffee on and make toast. I ate standing up, watching the sky lighten.

Someone entered the kitchen from the hall, and without turning around, I knew it was Jake. Maybe it was the masculine smell of the coal tar soap he favored, or maybe the sense of security that crept over me. That and desire.

I poured him a coffee, which he gulped scalding hot.

"I'm ready."

Cramming toast into his mouth, he swung out the door. I grabbed my bag and followed, throwing it into the back of the pickup amid rolls of fencing wire.

It seemed we bumped along red sand tracks forever. I stared out at the spinifex rings and the white gum trees that reminded me of bones. Clouds of dust billowed behind the pickup, and when Jake slowed for a washout, we were enveloped in a choking cloud. A mob of red kangaroos bounded alongside us, and Jake braked abruptly when its leader swerved in front of us. The pickup stalled.

Without the engine noise, I could appreciate how totally alone we were. I stared at Jake, seeing his sun-browned shoulders shift under his singlet. He was not a handsome man—too rugged, too tattered around the edges for that—but he was attractive. And sexual.

I put my hand on his thigh, just to see what he'd do. It was the first time I'd touched him in such a deliberate way.

"Christ, Sam," he said and reached for me, lunging over the gearstick to haul me close.

His hands were everywhere: running up my thigh and under my cutoff shorts to cup my ass, smoothing over my belly to stroke the underside of my breasts. Even through my thin cotton shirt they seared like branding irons.

His mouth teased my neck, his lips hot and slow in contrast to his fast, skimming hands. I tilted my head, trying to direct his mouth to mine, and when he finally slid over my cheek and claimed my mouth, I was already as stratospheric as the Southern Cross.

He kissed me deeply, his tongue delving in to stroke around my mouth. He tasted of cigarettes, dust, and coffee. "Chrissakes," he muttered, when his mouth lifted from mine. "The bloody gearstick's digging into me."

The blood thrummed in my veins. I ignored the offending gearstick and leaned across, pushing him back into his seat. I flicked open the snap on his shirt, bent, and trailed my lips down his rough, hairy chest.

He was right. This was too uncomfortable and probably too impossible.

I sat back, pressing a kiss to my fingertips and smoothing it over his lips. "Later, cowboy. We'll check out that bedroll of yours."

Frustration and irritation warred on his rocky face, then

he shrugged. "You're right, darl. I'll be harder and hotter for waiting."

For the next hour we drove in silence. My hand rested on Jake's thigh, and between frequent gear shifts for the rough track, he held my hand to his leg with casual possession.

During the heat of the day, I pretended to read my book, but really I watched Jake stride along the fence, stopping to bang in a post or tighten a wire. It was two hours before he returned, bringing with him the grassy smell of fresh sweat and a fine coating of red dust.

"Done," he said, and leaned over to kiss me hard.

My lips tingled. "Where will we camp?"

"Not far."

"Not far" was still an hour's drive through the bush. Jake stopped at the base of an escarpment, curved like the inside of a seashell, all red and ochre in a smooth unbroken wave.

Jake tossed the bedroll down under a gum tree. When next I looked, he was buck naked, pouring a billy can of water over his head. The liquid sluiced in rivulets down his back, winding through the dust to his firm, rounded buttocks.

I stood in the late afternoon sun looking...okay, *admiring* his body. For such a solid man he carried no surplus weight, and his bulky thighs and arms attested to physical work. He looked right in this environment, totally natural, as if the rugged landscape was somehow an extension of him.

Jake swung around and gave me a view of his chest and cock, which was as mouthwateringly solid and strong as the rest of him. He toweled carelessly with his discarded T-shirt before stepping back into his jeans. He caught me staring and grinned, shameless and smug.

I swatted a mosquito. "Do you always go commando?"

"Nope. Too uncomfortable most of the time. But I'll be

right for a while." He hoisted the billy. "You want a wash? I'll pour."

I hesitated. There was an intimacy involved that made me hesitate. This moved our relationship more than a single step; it pushed it to a familiarity I'd never attained with any other lover.

"Scared?"

"Not of you. More of what's going to bite me."

"You're making enough noise to scare off the snakes. As long as you stay out of the bull ants' nest, you'll be fine."

I was sweaty and dirty. Without stopping to consider further, I stripped off my clothes and marched over to Jake.

He hadn't moved. The can was still gripped in his hand, and the heat in his eyes could have scorched the already parched landscape into a conflagration.

The bulge in his jeans drew my eye, but I ignored it. "Well?"

I was deluged abruptly in a stream of water. I soaped and stood so that Jake could rinse me. This time, he poured the water slowly. Mindful of his gaze, I turned the rinse into a sensual self-caress, running my hands over my breasts, down my stomach, slowly, slowly between my legs, and along my thighs.

Jake put down the billy and hauled me into his arms His jeans were rough against my stomach and his chest hair abraded my breasts. His kiss was assured, a kiss which said he already knew the outcome of this. I wasn't going to argue.

My fingers snaked down to the soft skin above his jeans, before curling around to palm the bulge that swelled them. "You're overdressed."

He tugged me in the direction of the bedroll.

"Here?" I asked.

"Who's going to see us except a few birds? We've seen no one else all day."

My hesitation vanished. Suddenly, it seemed right, perfectly natural, to do this outdoors, under the bright blue sky, on the hard red ground. Australia was not a place for subtleties.

I shook off his hand and unsnapped his jeans, carefully lowering the zipper. His cock sprang free into the sunlight, hard, thick, and ready. I ran a finger from base to tip, passing over the moisture I found there.

Jake growled deep in his throat and kissed me again, his hands palming my breasts, fingers seeking my nipples. Somehow, we were on the sleeping bag, and his hands moved swiftly over my skin, curving around my hip for a moment before dipping between my legs.

I gasped. This was so quick, so urgent. If Jake had been one of my L.A. lovers, I'd have ordered him to slow down, directed his tongue to my nipples, not allowing him near my pussy until all the parameters of foreplay had been met. Somehow, though, as fast as Jake was going, I wanted him inside me as urgently as he obviously wanted to be there. This cowboy was in control; I was just hanging on for the ride. I fumbled for his cock and ran my fingers along its jutting length.

In turn, Jake's thick finger parted my sex and penetrated me, curling around to press on my pleasure point while his thumb stroked rhythmically on my clit. "Christ, Sam, you're so wet."

I gripped his cock tighter. "Then get inside me and make me even wetter."

He swung on top, and I parted my thighs to receive him. Dimly, I wondered when I'd last had sex in the missionary position. I like to be in control during sex. But here in the outback, with my life so totally in others' hands, I didn't consider arguing. Jake wanted control? He could have it. Besides, he felt damn good above me, his heavy body balanced on his elbows like a gentleman, his cock branding my belly.

I tilted my hips and he slid home in one smooth movement, then withdrew so that only the fat head of his cock was inside me. Another powerful thrust and he started a fierce pounding so intense that all I could do was grab his ass and hang on. I'd been poised at an acute level of arousal since he first kissed me, but now he took me to new heights. I closed my eyes, the better to focus on the feelings in my pussy, the sensation of being so fatly and completely filled, the steady rhythm, the ripples and shivers of impending climax.

"Look at me," Jake commanded. Sweat dripped from his face onto mine, and his blue eyes compelled me.

I locked gazes with him, dimly aware of the sunshine on my face, the caw of a crow. Then an extra deep thrust and my orgasm consumed me. I clenched down on his cock, arching and crying out with the intensity and power of each burst of pleasure.

He was still hard inside me, his movements only a gentle rocking. I felt boneless and so wet that I wondered if he could feel anything in my pussy. He smiled, leaned to kiss me, and started again, with deep thrusts that felt so damn *good* I wondered for a breathless moment if I was going to come again.

I clenched down on his cock and was rewarded by his hoarse cry as his cock twitched and spilled inside me.

And then it was over. Jake moved up and took me in his arms, rolling so that I lay over his chest. His heart pounded a steady rhythm.

It was a long, lazy night. Jake cooked steak and potatoes on the campfire and produced beer from the cooler. The moon rose early, painting the landscape with a silver glow. We sat and listened to the night birds and the thump of a kangaroo before moving to the bedroll to make love again. Softer, sweet love, less desperate than before but no less satisfying.

We were both up early the next morning. It was one of those breathless outback mornings when the light is so clear and sharp it hurts your eyes and the birdsong is a glorious chorus.

Jake had tossed the bedroll onto the back of the pickup and was shoveling sand over the campfire when he stiffened. "Got company." Along the track, a cloud of dust moved fast in our direction.

"Probably someone from the station," I said.

"Doubt it. Probably those Americans who were looking for you."

I'd managed to forget about them. Instantly, it all came rushing back. I shot a glance at Jake, wondering if I should tell him.

A white Toyota slid to a stop in the dust, and three men got out. They weren't local, that much I could tell by their clothes.

"Can I help you?" Jake asked. His laconic drawl belied his tight posture.

"We're okay," said one of the men. "We were looking for our little cousin Samantha from Los Angeles, and I reckon we've just found her."

"I don't know you," I said, looking from one to the other. Then the third man moved around the Toyota into view, and I gasped. It was Agent Dolan.

"Hello Sam," he said. "You're difficult to track down. Grab your things, we're outta here."

"We're going back to L.A.?"

"Yeah. So say goodbye to your friend, and we'll be off."

I glanced at Jake. There was an icy stillness about him that was unnerving. I went across to him.

"I'm sorry," I said, "but I can't explain. It's sorta complicated." Rising on tiptoes, I kissed his mouth.

He grabbed me by the waist and kissed me deeply, breaking

the kiss to lean his forehead against mine. "Sam," he breathed against my lips. "Try and trust me on this." His grip tightened around my waist. "She doesn't want to go with you." His tone was altered from his usual mellow drawl; it was hard, cold—the voice of a different man.

The hairs rose on the back of my neck. "I have to—"

"Shut the hell up, Sam, and do as I say."

I hesitated. Something was very wrong here. Why was Jake behaving so strangely? And why had Agent Dolan appeared here instead of waiting at the homestead until I returned? I frowned, trying to piece together what was wrong, what *felt* wrong. Then it hit me. The Americans hadn't known where I was. Agent Dolan should have known where to find me. Why had they gone to Avoca Downs yesterday?

I shrugged, feigning casualness. "We'll have to go back to Malory to get my stuff. I'll ride along with Jake and see you there."

"There's no time for that, Sam." Agent Dolan came closer.

Jake grabbed my arm and shoved, and I went sprawling into the pickup.

"What are you doing?" I struggled to sit up and pushed my hair out of my eyes.

Jake leaped into the driver's seat, turning the key and slamming the pickup into gear in one movement. "Shut up." Dust and small stones sprayed behind the wheels as he gunned the engine.

I stared across at him, fear leaping into my mouth with a metallic taste.

I swallowed over the pounding of my heart. "Where are you taking me?"

"Sam, I know you're scared, but you have to trust me on this. Right now, I have to get us away from here alive."

"Alive?" My voice squeaked, and suddenly there wasn't enough air in the cab. "What do you mean?"

A noise registered over the roaring engine, a noise I'd heard a time or two in L.A. Gunshots.

"They're shooting at us! But that's—" I gathered my thoughts still unable to make a leap of trust and confide in Jake.

The pickup fishtailed wildly as Jake rounded a bend on the dusty track. Another shot sounded.

"Get down, Sam."

I stared at him. He was a jackaroo, a cowboy. What the hell did he know about guns and how to drive as if the hounds of hell were after him?

"Sam." His voice was clipped, the laconic drawl gone. "Get the fuck down before the next shot sprays your brains over the dash."

I slid lower, crouching like an air passenger on crash drill. But I could still hear the noise, the hammering pursuit, and it was worse not knowing.

"We're going off road. Only way to shake them."

I gripped the armrest as I was jostled even harder. Jake swerved away from the track, avoiding rocks and larger clumps of spinifex, plowing through the smaller ones. The smell of burnt vegetation filled the cab.

"They're the drug lords you're hiding from."

The pickup careened over a washout, dropping with a thud onto its springs.

"But Agent Dolan brought me here."

"There is no Agent Dolan. That man is not an FBI agent, whatever you might think. Now shut up and let me drive."

Fear and dust coated my mouth, and for the first time I wondered if I was going to make it out alive. I didn't know much about Jake, but his words had a solidity to them that reassured me. I decided to trust him. Right now, I didn't have any other option.

I glanced back. It was hard to see over the bouncing rolls of fencing wire in the back of the pickup, but then I got a clear view.

"Jake, they're on fire!"

Flames shot out from the side of the Toyota, and the smoke rolled thick and dark.

Jake glanced at the mirror. "Spinifex must have got trapped on the chassis and caught alight from the exhaust. This will give us a chance." He didn't slow his cracking pace.

The Toyota slowed as flames engulfed its rear.

"She'll blow," Jake muttered, but he didn't slow down. "The fuel tanks won't last."

The Toyota's doors opened, and it came to a rocking halt. I could see Agent Dolan scrambling out, but he'd barely taken one pace when the explosion boomed, a giant fireball rising to the sky.

Jake stopped. Agent Dolan lay face down, but even from a distance it was obvious he was dead. Of the other two men, there was no sign.

I started to shake, a fine tremor in my hands that wouldn't stop. Three men were dead, I was alive, and the topsy-turvy world I'd been living in for the past week had just taken another quarter turn. I buried my face in my trembling hands and waited for the nausea to pass.

Long minutes later, when I trusted my voice not to waver, I looked over at Jake. "What happens now?"

We made camp an hour later. I wanted to be far enough away from the Toyota that I couldn't see or smell anything. We made soft, sweet love on the bedroll, a slow merging of our bodies.

When it was over, I cried big gulping sobs. Jake held me close to his chest and didn't say anything.

It was much later, after we'd eaten, that I turned to Jake and said. "Tell me."

"I was sent to Malory to look out for you."

"You're not a jackaroo?"

"I am. I work on a station about three hours south of here. But I also work for ASIO—the Australian equivalent of your FBI.

"Dolan contacted you in L.A., posing as a FBI agent, and spun you a story about the witness protection program. But he worked for the cartel—they wanted you out of the way."

"Why not just kill me?"

Jake looked down at his dusty boots. "You were a hostage. While the real FBI hunted for you and tried to negotiate your release, the gang went to ground. The FBI finally located you here, and that's when ASIO became involved. It was my job to gain your trust and get you out before the cartel came to get you. A few days ago, the FBI arrested the main players in L.A. That's when the cartel came looking—but they couldn't find you, so they brought Dolan back."

I sat, silently digesting what he'd said. "So the people at Malory work for the cartel?"

"No. They genuinely thought they were helping the FBI. There are stations here that take people on the witness protection program."

My life had been turned upside down for a lie. And Jake was a lie too. I tried to feel anger at how he'd seduced me, but all I felt was sadness. "Is Jake your real name?"

"Yeah."

"And seducing me was part of keeping me safe?"

"*No!*" For a big man he moved swiftly, and he crouched in

the dirt next to me. "Don't think that, Sam. That was very definitely not supposed to happen. But you're smart and sexy, and I like you. *More* than like you, if you must know."

I searched his face, hunting for the truth.

Jake stared back, a half smile on his face. "Do you believe me?"

"I do." And I did.

Later, when the kissing had stopped, when we were sticky and sated once more, I asked, "What happens now?"

"We get dressed. We're expected back at Malory Station."

I had to ask. "And after that?"

He touched my face. "That's up to you. You'll have to return to L.A. for the trial. But after that..." His eyes were clear and blue. "Maybe you'll come back and find me."

BANGING THE COWBOY

Randi Alexander

Annie Paris watched him from the stage, stealing peeks from behind the concealment of her cymbals as she banged out the rhythm to a Brad Paisley song.

Rafe McCord. God, he was big. The Big Cowboy, women called him. And one lucky girl was tight in his arms right now, two-stepping around the scarred wooden dance floor.

Almost missing her cue, Annie slid into a four-measure drum solo. When she'd finished, the lead guitarist/singer—her cousin Shawn—told the crowd, "On percussion, Annie Paris!" Polite applause sounded here and there around the room like the first pellets of a hailstorm.

She twirled one drumstick over her head and smiled a thank you, then went right back into the groove. After introducing the rest of the band, Shawn announced, "We're gonna take a fifteen minute pause for the cause, folks. Stick around for the last set."

She stood and scanned the crowd, but her glance caught on

one stare from the bar. Rafe. Looking at her? A jingle of desire vibrated through her, making her heart thud as she gazed back into dark eyes shaded by a black Stetson.

He was tall, but the name Big Cowboy came from his muscles. Tonight his broad shoulders and massive arms were clothed in a light plaid western-cut shirt he'd probably had to buy from a bodybuilders' store.

He raised his longneck in salute, which made things even hotter low in her belly, deep in her pussy. But she looked away. It was one thing to crush on a cowboy, but quite another to act on it.

Annie grabbed her water glass and headed to the bar for a refill, but the thirsty crowd was three-deep. The only opening was the server's station, right where Rafe had planted himself in his usual spot.

Her steps slowed as she caught his gaze. Had he been watching her the whole time? Pasting on a smile, she stepped up to the open spot. "Hey, Rafe." They'd talked a number of times in the last year—her band played here the second weekend of every month. The sexual tension had always been thick between them, but tonight it was downright palpable, setting her knees to wobbling and her core to quivering.

"Evenin', Miss Annie," he drawled, and touched the brim of his hat. That smoky voice sent heat to places between her thighs that had no business responding to him. She didn't look down, but she knew her tingling nipples were hard and jutting, obvious for everyone to see through her lacy bra and pink silk tank top. Obvious for Rafe to see.

As the bartender refilled her glass with ice water, she looked at Rafe and let herself drift away under the spell of his beautiful, dark brown eyes. Nine months ago she'd been sure she was falling in love with him. They'd flirted a dozen or so times. She'd been confused as to why he'd never asked her out.

Then one night she found out why. In the ladies' room. She was in a stall, just zipping up her jeans, when she heard two women come in.

"He's gorgeous," a southern accent twanged. "I can see why you warned me away from him. You want him all to yourself."

"True. But that's not the main reason," a sultry voice purred. "He likes it...rough."

"Really? Yeah, I can see that. He's so big."

"They call him The Big Cowboy, but his name is Rafe." She sighed. "He's so damn good, I can't get him out of my mind. But we only had that one night."

"If he's so good, why don't you just grab him and drag him home?"

Another sigh. "I've tried. But it's not by my choice. He's turned me down a couple of times already. Very nicely. He's a gentleman...until he gets you naked. Then he's all man." She walked to the stall next to Annie's and closed the door.

The twangy woman called, "Well, rough sex isn't for me, so don't worry. If he talks to me, I'll give him the freeze out."

From the stall, the woman laughed, "He won't ask you out. That's his thing. He never asks—he makes women come to him."

"Serious?"

"Uh huh." She flushed and opened the door. "Word has spread, and women hang all over him. He has his pick every night."

The women left, and Annie stood immobile. Although the thought of rough sex with Rafe did something naughty to her body, she'd backed off, smothering the fire he'd started inside her.

She wasn't a one-night-stand kind of girl. She was looking

for more, and it would have killed her to make love to him and then have to watch him take home a different girl every time her band played here.

But sometimes she wished she'd listened to her body instead of her heart that night. She would have asked him to come home with her, and then she would have known what it was like to be taken by the sexiest man she'd ever met.

"Annie?" Rafe was smiling. A killer cowboy grin that sent tingles across her flesh.

"Huh?" she asked, blinking out of her trance.

"I asked," he said kindly, "how things are going tonight."

"Oh, yeah. Good." Brilliant. "You?"

"No complaints."

Before she could compose an intelligent sentence, a tall, leggy redhead sidled up behind him and put her arms around his waist. He turned.

Damn. Annie crossed the empty dance floor and set her glass on the stage as she passed, then scooted into the bathroom. Her face in the mirror was stoplight red.

Goddamn, that man made her moist. Hot and throbbing. Sent her halfway to an orgasm with just his voice, his eyes. And she wanted it rough. Nine months of fantasizing had brought her close to obsession. What sexy things would he do to her? And what wicked things would he let her do to him?

But it wasn't going to happen with Rafe. She wouldn't risk it. She'd just keep dating guys from church and friends of her friends' boyfriends, and one day she'd find someone who wanted her love as well as her body.

Finishing up, she walked out of the bathroom and climbed the three steps onto the stage. She tried to avoid looking at Rafe. Didn't want to see him with another woman when she wanted to be the one wrapped around him. But she was unable to resist one quick glance. Oh, God. He was alone. And he was watching her.

The distance between them seemed to shrink, the sounds of the bar fading to white noise. Yes, damn it, she wanted to sample his rough loving, wanted his big body flattening her against a wall, kissing her savagely as his hand tweaked her nipple, pulling and twisting just hard enough to make her cry in ecstasy. Lifting her legs with his big, calloused hands, sliding his hard cock into her dripping pussy. A hard fuck. A fast bang, both of them grunting as they slammed their hips together, deeper and faster...

"Annie!" A spritz of water hit her face from her cousin's fingers. "Your water." He held out the glass. "Where the hell were you just now?"

She took the cold, sweating glass, pressed it to her cheek and thought fast. "Grocery list."

"Right. More'n likely you were pickin' out a cowboy to take home." He walked away.

Annie shook her head and sat on her drum throne, adjusted her snare and high-hat, then dug out her drumsticks.

It'd been too long since she'd brought anyone home. And the only cowboy she wanted in her bed was Rafe. The guys she dated were nice, maybe even boyfriend material, but there was never any spark.

The next set was a leisurely one, getting people out to slow dance, mellowing them down so there wouldn't be any fights outside the bar. Rafe danced with a few women, each of them sashaying up to him and brazenly offering themselves.

But when each dance was over, Rafe walked his partner back to her table and left her to head back to his spot at the bar—standing alone again until the next woman gave it a try.

By the end of the set, Annie was watching him so intently,

she flubbed a transition. Shawn grinned at her, and said into the mic, "Our little Annie here, isn't paying attention." He winked at her, then scanned the crowd. "Which makes me think…"

He wouldn't…

"She's trying to decide who to bring home with her tonight. All you single cowboys out there…"

"No." Her eyes opened wide.

"She's single. And has her own apartment with a king-sized bed."

Oh. Fuck. She closed her eyes and tapped along to the last song as shouts of "Yee-haw," and "Show us your tits," and "Annie get *my* gun" reached her.

Her cousin grinned.

Using one drumstick poking out of her fist, Annie flipped him off—drummer style. But all he did was laugh.

As the song finished, he thanked everyone and gave them a "Drive safe, folks," and then the band started packing up.

Annie folded the legs on her throne and set it aside. She started unscrewing the wingnut holding her ride symbol on its stand, but stopped, sensing someone behind her. She turned and nearly tripped on the base drum petal. "Rafe?"

When he stood this close, she could see the faint scar that slashed his cheek and smell his aftershave, dark and mysterious. Just like him. Then his lips curved into a seductive grin, making her insides shimmy, amping up her desire until it was painful to keep from touching him.

"So. You're single with a king-sized bed, huh?"

She blinked a few times.

He bent and picked up her throne, then grabbed her floor tom. "Your van's out back?"

She nodded, amazed he was helping, but even more so that he knew she had a van and where she'd parked it.

"Unlocked?"

Another stunned-speechless nod from her.

He gave a quiet laugh and walked off, his heavy thighs bunching as he went down the steps, his boots thudding heavily on the wood. All she could do was stare at his ass.

She unfastened everything and picked up the bass drum just as he came back. He took it, and as their fingers brushed, their gazes locked. His nostrils flared, and she imagined him doing the same thing as he moved his head between her spread thighs, looking at her over her mound as he breathed in her woman scent. His lips would open and his tongue would find her secret place, exploring, licking, kissing. "Oh, yes."

"Yes?" he said with a wily grin.

Had she just moaned that out loud? Shit. "Yes, thank you for helping."

His chuckle was pure cowboy as he walked off the stage and out the door.

On the last trip, they walked out together. This side of the lot was nearly empty now, and as she closed the back doors of her van she sensed him behind her again. "Thank you, Rafe. I appreciate the help."

Okay, now was her chance. She could just invite him home with her. Let him know that she was okay with—no, *craved*— his rough loving. That, in fact, it turned her on to the point where she could smell her own pussy juices flowing from her cunt. But just one night? Could she be satisfied with that?

She turned to face him, opening her mouth, not sure what she was going to say, but he spoke first.

"Annie, I was hoping you'd..." There was a long pause.

She leaned back on the van for support. "Yes?"

He stuffed his hands in his front pockets and tipped his head down.

Oh. My. God. Was he nervous? A tiny whimper escaped her. She'd never seen this side of him. Never imagined he had a side that was introverted. She wanted to go to him, hold him around the waist, look up into his eyes, and kiss away his doubts.

But she stayed where she was. Hoping she was reading the situation correctly. Hoping he wasn't about to ask her for drum lessons or to borrow her van.

His chest rose and fell with a deep breath, then he looked at her. "Would you like to go someplace for coffee?"

"Coffee?" Okay, so it wasn't an invitation to his house by the river where he'd toss her on his bed and ram his cock into her until they both screamed with ecstasy. "Coffee?" she repeated. Stupidly.

He pulled his hands out of his pockets and squared his shoulders.

Annie waited for the rest.

"I want to ask you out." His jaw worked, then he added, "On a date."

"A date?" Things weren't filtering through her brain, they were just going directly from her ears to her mouth and out.

He chuckled. "Yeah, like dinner and a movie."

She sunk slowly to sit on the van's bumper, not trusting her knees to hold her up. "I'm a little confused." She shook her head. "I mean, from what I've heard..." Oh, shit. She hadn't meant to say that.

He took off his hat. Almost as if he was just remembering his manners. "I know what you've heard. And about half the rumors are true." Smacking his Stetson on his leg, he asked, "Do you think you could ignore all that and go out with me sometime?"

This was so much farther than any of her fantasies ever took her. A date, a real opportunity to have the Big Cowboy, Rafe, in her life. Using her hands as leverage, she pushed up and walked to him, every nerve in her body on edge, wanting him, wanting all of him. *Right now.* No waiting for some future date night. She would make the first move tonight. If he was brave enough to ask her for a date, she'd be brave enough to go after what she wanted.

Standing toe to toe with him, she placed her palms on his chest. Her skin met warm flesh over hard, sculpted muscles, and it sent shivers through her. "Yes, Rafe. I'd like to date you." *Deep breath. Work up the courage.* "But I want you tonight, too."

His eyes widened then narrowed—and then he moved, walking her backward and pressing her against the van door. He reached up and set his hat on the roof, then stroked a hand down her hair, across her jaw line, ran his calloused thumb across her lips. "I want you, Annie." His voice was rough, like dry gravel. "I've wanted you since that first day, almost a year ago."

"Then why didn't you—"

He cut her off with his mouth. A gentle kiss, and he groaned as his tongue parted her lips, teasing her slowly.

Everything became sensory. All thoughts disappeared as her nipples, hard and sensitized, pressed against his chest, sending tingles of need through her. And against her belly, she could feel his hard cock burning through his denim and her silk.

Her hands ranged over him, across the bulky muscles of his shoulders, up the nape of his neck to the sexy cowlick in his short hair. Her core convulsed, needing more, ready to take him in, and a flush of heat flowed through her veins.

Then the kiss deepened, and his tongue stroked hers, circled it, then sucked it gently into his mouth where she tasted the insides of his lips and traced the edges of his teeth.

He shifted his body, put his hands on her ass, lifted her off the ground, and pressed her back against the van. Then he moved, grinding his hard shaft against her mound, hitting her clit through her jeans at the perfect angle. With each pass, lightning strikes of pure desire rattled through her core and up her spine, melting her brain cells as she drew close to an orgasm.

She moaned, then whimpered. God, was there room in the back of her van for this big man? She'd be willing to dump her drums onto the pavement...

"My place or yours?" he asked, pausing the sweet, naughty grinding.

Panting, she tried to focus on his question. He lived a mile and a half out of town in the foreman's house on a big ranch. She lived five minutes away... "My house," she blurted, sounding trampy but not caring.

He eased her down, grabbed his hat, and held out his hand. "Keys."

They reached her place quickly—a little one-bedroom above an insurance office that was closed evenings and weekends. Perfect for a drummer. Or for a wild night of loud, rough sex.

She fumbled the door keys, then got the damn thing open. He slammed it shut behind them. The space was small, just a landing with steps that led up to her apartment.

He pulled her into his arms and his kiss devastated her. Overwhelmed her. She had to remember to breathe as he explored her mouth, touching, tasting everywhere. He bit her lips gently, and she bit him back not so gently.

Her pussy quivered, juicing and contracting, every thought in her brain centering on how to end the torture, how to get him deep inside her. Her nipples pulsed with her racing heartbeat, needing his touch, his lips, his teeth.

Then he stepped back, panting, his eyes nearly black with

passion, his jaw set and his lips hard and flat. "Are you sure, Annie? I can stop now, but once I get you naked—"

"I'm sure," she breathed, then pulled her top up and off, not caring how wild that made her look.

Rafe ripped at the snaps of his cowboy shirt, yanking it off to reveal a perfect chest with a sprinkling of dark hair across his pecs, over his taut abs, and down into his jeans, which strained with his erection.

She reached out and stroked his chest, then moved lower, cupping his cock through the denim.

He jerked and howled, and she felt the power of his desire surge through her. Unbuckling, unsnapping, and unzipping, she freed him, and in her hand, the Big Cowboy became massive.

"I want you inside me," she groaned, looking into his eyes and seeing fierce, untamed lust. She pulled his jeans down, kneeling in front of him to take off his boots, rendering him completely naked. Then she moved her face closer to his cock.

It bobbed with each powerful heartbeat, and she needed to taste him. Circling the base with one hand and holding his balls with the other, she licked his head, tasting pre-come in the slit. "What do you want now, Rafe?" she asked, energized with the power she held over him.

He bared his teeth and made a feral noise. "Suck it."

That's what she wanted to hear. And she did what he asked, taking it all in, swallowing his big cock deep. The circumference was more than she'd ever had, and it strained her jaw. But she sucked, swallowed him, pulled back, and breathed, taking as much pleasure herself in this domination as she gave him.

"Baby," he groaned. "You have to stop or I won't be able to." He lifted her from under her arms, then kissed her slowly, almost with worship. "That," he whispered against her lips, "was outstanding."

"More?" she asked with a smile.

"Uh uh. I want to fuck you, hard and fast."

A thrill shimmied through her as her pussy clenched and a wave of heat raced through her. "I want that, Rafe. *Now.*"

He undressed her, wasting no time on finesse, then turned her over. "Put your hands on the steps."

She bent and obeyed, then looked over her shoulder at him.

Staring at her ass, and lower, at her pussy, his eyes were slits, his nostrils flared, just as she'd fantasized.

"Kiss me," she begged, wanting him between her legs.

He immediately went to one knee and grabbed her thighs, then softened the grip and ran his hands up her legs, over the round cheeks of her ass, and back down to her calves. Then he kissed her pussy, so gently it could have been his breath, but then with more passion, more force. He kissed and licked, nibbled and sucked, until her clit throbbed, wanting him, begging for him.

"Rafe, please."

"Not yet, beautiful. I want to be inside you when you come."

She heard rustling, the snap of latex, and then he was standing behind her. "Hang onto the railing."

She moved her hand to get a firm grip.

"Now the other hand. Around my neck."

She reached back to do as he asked, excited to see what position they were moving into.

His hand eased down between her legs and took her by the knee, and he eased her leg up. He spread her, lifting her leg, holding it with the crook of his arm around the back of her knee, her other leg straight, her foot on the floor.

Annie felt so open, so vulnerable, but she loved every second of it.

"That's it, baby, relax. Relax and get your sweet pussy ready for me."

His voice rumbled over her, through her, starting her core contracting again and her heart racing.

"Aw, Annie," he said quietly as his cock found the opening to her cunt, and he positioned himself at her entry.

"Hard and fast, Rafe. Please," she begged, feeling her pussy juices running down the inside of her thigh.

Then he did it, rammed home, one sure, strong stroke, and he was buried inside her.

She shrieked, the pleasure overriding the sweet sting of his huge cock in her tight passage.

"Okay?" he asked, not moving except for the shaking in his limbs and the pulsing of his rod deep inside her.

"Yes," she sighed. "More. Harder."

His growl echoed in the small space and he grabbed her hair, tugging lightly.

"Yes. Harder."

He obeyed, and the nip of pain accelerated her race toward completion. "God, Rafe. I like it rough. Make me feel it."

His hips jerked, and he eased his cock out of her, only to ram it in again, pumping out, then back in, deeper this time. Each stroke was faster than the last, harder, deeper inside her.

Annie's body gloried in the feel of him inside her. Her legs stretched to accommodate him, his hold on her hair sending a tingling through her scalp. His cock rammed into her, the friction in her pussy growing hotter, bolder, until she felt herself starting to fly.

Rafe let go of her hair and slid a finger into her mound, finding her clit and rubbing fast in rhythm with his fucking.

"Yes," she screamed, as ecstasy flowed through her body, hot and dark, spinning her mind as flecks of light pierced her eyelids and a high, keening cry escaped her throat. It slowed, and she felt herself drifting down, closer to reality. Rafe adjusted the two of them, placing her hands on the step again, her feet on the floor, spread for his pleasure.

He moved again, thrusting into her, grunting as he pushed in deeper.

Annie cried in delight, then let loose a shout of surprise when he pinched her clit between his fingers, sending her over the top again, spiraling through space, spinning her reality until she didn't know where she was.

But he was there, behind her, holding her, his chest pressed against her back, one hand on the step above hers, the other around her waist. She panted, her head hanging from her shoulders, no muscle left in her body.

Then he drove in again, his hips slapping against hers as he rammed, deep and fast, into her quivering core. His lips pressed to her shoulder, then his teeth caught her as a shout wrenched from him and he pistoned in and out as fast as his heart pounded. With one last plunge into her, he shouted, "Annie, baby."

He collapsed as best he could, his body shuddering as his heartbeat thudded against her back.

They both took a moment to breathe, to come back to normal—if she'd ever want to be normal again. Then he kissed her shoulder and stood, taking her with him, and turned her to hold her close, stroking her hair as she dangled limply in his arms.

Without warning, he picked her up and trudged up the stairs.

She looked up into his face. "Wow."

He chuckled. "Yeah, wow. Amazing."

Stroking his jaw, she asked, "Good for you?"

His eyes fired with intensity. "Better than good."

What was he trying to say with his eyes that he couldn't say with his mouth?

He found her bedroom and laid her on the quilt, leaning over her with a hand on either side of her shoulders. "Can I stay?" he asked, suddenly looking unsure.

"Yes. I want you here all night." She wrapped her arms around his neck and pulled him down next to her. "Then tomorrow we can..." Oh, crap, was that too much? She bit her lower lip.

He stroked her breasts, gently, reverently. "Tomorrow, we'll go out to my place, sit on the porch and watch the river run past." He smiled. "Between bouts of lovemaking."

Lovemaking? Her heart shuffled in her chest. This wasn't sex, this was something more. He'd invited her to his house. And he wanted to date her. A smile burst across her face before she could stop it.

"And what are you grinning about?" he asked, still caressing her breasts.

"I can't seem to figure out..."

"Hmm?" His fingers tweaked her nipples.

"Why I didn't grab you up nine months ago."

He stopped and looked into her eyes. "I'm glad you didn't."

"Why?" Her breath caught at the serious look in his eyes.

Taking her hand, he moved it to his chest. "It took me this long to figure out what this is."

Annie looked at their hands, pressed together over his heart, and sweet, tender emotion brought tears to her eyes. "Rafe?" She couldn't believe this was happening.

"It's my heart, Annie." His brow furrowed, his eyes glittered. "And it beats for you."

"Are you sure?" What an awful question, but she had to find out why. "How do you know?"

He smiled and released her hand. "When I woke up this

morning, the last year caught up with me. I realized I couldn't wait to see you tonight. And I've never felt that way about a woman. Before you." Her eyes flooded with tears as happiness choked her. She had it all, now. A rough-riding man whose heart was as gentle as a country love song. She touched his cheek. "Kiss me, cowboy."

LADIES LOVE COUNTRY BOYS

Cat Johnson

N o, no, no. Please don't do this to me." Shaking, Julia
Craven realized the power brakes and power steering
weren't working. She fought to control the vehicle as the rental
car ignored her pleas. It coasted and eventually slowed to a stop
on the shoulder of the highway.

Pulse racing, she threw the gearshift into park. She twisted
the key in the ignition, but got no response. She turned the key
again. Still no response.

"Dammit!" Julia smacked the steering wheel with the palm
of one hand and tried to think of what to do next.

After flipping on the hazard lights, she leaned over and
grabbed the rental agreement from the glove compartment. By
the light of her cell phone she located a phone number printed
on the paperwork and dialed. She had to explain the situation
to three different people before she reached someone who could
help her.

"I can call a tow truck, but it could take an hour or two to get him there." The soothing Texas drawl of the woman on the phone seemed far less comforting as she delivered that information.

"Two hours?" Julia glanced at the clock on the dash. She let out a huff of frustration. "Fine. What about a replacement vehicle? I need to get back to my hotel, and then to the airport first thing in the morning."

"Oh, I don't know when I'd be able to get one out to you. It's Friday night."

"Yes, I realize that." If only Julia's client, who'd scheduled the dinner meeting in the outskirts of Austin, had also been so aware of the day and time. "Can you at least call a taxi to get me back to the hotel?"

"I'll see what I can do, but there's a huge festival in Austin this week. It's nearly impossible to find an available cab in the city. Forget about getting one to come out to where you are. It could take a while."

"What am I supposed to do in the meantime?" The thought of sitting alone in the car on the dark highway, even with the doors locked, was starting to freak Julia out.

"Is there somewhere you can wait until the tow truck arrives?"

There was nothing behind her, but she did see lights, and even a Ferris wheel, ahead. "It looks like there's a fair maybe a quarter mile up the road. I guess I could walk there."

"Good. I have the GPS location of the vehicle and your cell phone number. I'll give you a call when the driver arrives."

Thinking she'd just have to make the best of a bad situation, Julia thanked the woman and hung up. She grabbed her bag, locked the car, and started walking.

By the time she'd reached the source of the lights, her feet hurt, the shoes she'd paid far too much for were scuffed and dusty, and she'd cursed her unreliable vehicle at least a dozen times. As she stumbled to the entrance, the first sign that greeted her read RODEO AUSTIN. There was no attendant in the booth, so she pushed through the turnstile and entered the fairgrounds to see the brightly lit words COLD BEER.

Tired and thirsty, Julia made a beeline for the vendor beneath the sign. A quick exchange of words, cash, and one big plastic cup, and soon cold frothy brew slipped down Julia's parched throat. She probably sucked it down faster than she should have, but with the night she was having, she needed it.

Might as well see the sights while I'm here, she thought. At least it would make for a good story when she got back to the office: Julia's Great Austin Adventure.

"So what goes on around here?" she asked the beer vendor. "I've never been to a rodeo before."

"The events are almost over, but if you hurry you can still catch the tail end." The server tilted her head toward the building next to the booth.

Cup in hand, although it was a lot less full now, Julia wandered toward the source of the noise and action. She looked over the railing and down at the dirt-covered arena. The announcer's voice echoed over the crowd, informing the cheering crowd of a score she didn't understand the significance of.

It was the view that really grabbed her attention. Her gaze settled on a line of cowboys. They sat on the top of a rail, facing the arena and laughing as they watched a man dressed in clown makeup dancing to music. The buffet of jeans-clad butts and strong thighs covered in chaps was entrancing. Julia took another sip of beer, but it couldn't quench the particular thirst the view caused deep inside.

Who knew she had a cowboy fetish? Certainly not Julia. Then again, when had she ever had the opportunity to see so many up close and personal? Never.

One man in the group glanced away from the action and up toward Julia. From beneath the cowboy hat, his gaze met and held hers. Julia swallowed hard, suddenly dry-mouthed in spite of the beer.

Speaking of up close and personal... She wouldn't mind getting that way with him.

She'd been caught staring, but try as she might Julia couldn't break eye contact. In fact, she might have forgotten to breathe for a bit.

He smiled, making him look both devilish and amused. It sent her heart fluttering. When he winked at her, her knees nearly buckled. Then he hopped down from the railing, and she lost sight of him.

She pressed closer to the railing, bobbing her head to see past the row of cowboys closing around her tall, dark and handsome hottie. There was lots of movement, but all she saw was the top of his black hat.

What was going on down there inside that tiny, railed-in enclosure? More importantly, when would it be over so she could get back to ogling her new fantasy man? Julia didn't have a clue, and the announcer's babble about chutes and numbers and percentages wasn't answering her questions either.

Frustrated in more ways than one, Julia took another sip of beer. She nearly choked mid-swallow when the gate of the enclosure crashed open and her cowboy bolted out atop a bucking, spinning—not to mention huge and horned—bull.

The cowboy somehow managed to hang on through all the twists and turns the animal made. She watched in amazement, torn between fear for his life and lust for his body. What was it that had her melting inside from just watching this man do the most asinine thing she'd ever seen?

The cowboy leapt off the beast and landed on his shoulder in the dust, inches from deadly-looking hooves. He scrambled to his feet just as the animal turned back to chase him.

Wide-eyed and unable to look away, Julia watched it all.

Why did this dirt-covered, insane cowboy fascinate her so? Up until now, only pristinely dressed, high-powered businessmen in Armani suits had broken through her sexual walls. This cowboy was making her feel like no other man ever had.

Why was that? He rode bulls, for God's sake, and yet she was turned on enough to rip those dust-covered clothes from his body and jump him right here. Maybe it was just the sheer testosterone-fueled manliness of him. Some long-forgotten cave-woman instinct telling her body he'd be a good mate.

Her twenty-first-century woman's intuition was definitely thinking he'd be a good bedmate, even as the logical part of her brain tried to convince her that wanting to jump a stranger while stranded at a Texas rodeo was crazy.

Telling her conscience to shut up, Julia took another long sip of beer and emptied the cup. One refill and she'd probably be dropping her designer panties for the sexy stranger behind the building like a horny teenager. A teenager, she was not. Horny, on the other hand...

She threw the cup in a garbage can as she tracked his progress across the arena floor. No, it wasn't the alcohol making her feel like this. The complete drought of eligible, desirable men in her life, maybe, but not the beer.

He exited the arena floor through a gate, but she could still see him through the railings. Grinning, he accepted a slap on the back and a handshake from another cowboy. Julia stifled a groan as she imagined what those big, rough hands would feel like caressing her bare skin.

She was really getting into the fantasy when she heard the

ringing inside her bag and scrambled to find her cell phone. "Hello?"

"Good news. The tow truck will be there in an hour, and I can have a replacement rental dropped off at the garage where your car's being towed by the time you get there."

"That's great. Thank you so much." Julie disconnected with a sigh of relief. With those two worries off her mind, she could go back to enjoying her cowboy fantasy until it was time to go meet the tow truck.

Her gaze swept the area where the cowboys were hanging out, but the black hat she sought was nowhere to be found. Julia expanded her visual search, taking in the action happening across from her where a different cowboy was straddling the rails, about to lower himself onto another bull. She still didn't see the one man she wanted.

Frowning, Julia fought the pout threatening to settle on her lips.

"A pretty lady should never drink alone."

The deep, soul-stirring drawl was accompanied by a cup of beer thrust in front of her. Julia's chest tightened as she took the offered beverage and slowly turned toward the man handing it to her.

His eyes beneath the black brim of the hat were so blue she actually looked closer to see if they were colored contacts. They weren't. Everything about this man was real—his sun-browned skin, the dirt streaking one cheek, even the deep laugh lines that crinkled the corners of those gorgeous eyes when he smiled down at her.

Julia swallowed the dryness from her throat. "Thank you."

"My pleasure, Miss..."

"Julia." She supplied her first name only and tried not to spill her beer as her hands began to shake.

"Miss Julia." He tipped his hat. "I'm Morgan Mitchell, but you already know that."

"I do?" She raised a brow in question. Julia was fairly certain she'd never met him before. A woman simply didn't forget a man like this.

"The announcer." He laughed as she frowned and continued to wonder what he was talking about. "They announced my name when I rode just now."

"Oh. Of course." She wasn't about to admit she'd been too busy imagining him naked to listen to the announcer. "Sorry, it's hard to hear in here."

He nodded and sipped at his own beer. His gaze dropped, down to the high-heeled pumps so out of place at a rodeo, then back up past her pencil skirt and button-down shirt to finally settle on her face. "So what brings a city girl like you to Rodeo Austin?"

She didn't bother asking why he'd assume she was a *city girl*, as he'd put it. Julia considered telling him about her meeting and the rental car debacle, but as the clock ticked closer to her impending departure time, she decided against it. If she had to play Cinderella and catch the next tow truck home by midnight, she was taking some memories with her. "Maybe I came looking for a cowboy."

Morgan's brows rose high enough to meet the dark shock of hair peeking from beneath his hat. "Well then, you came to the right place. You, uh, looking for one in particular? Or will I do?"

Need twisted low in her belly. "I think you'll do just fine."

His eyes narrowed. She met his stare with a bold one of her own. If he was wondering whether she was serious, he could stop. She'd never been more sincere. Julia hadn't gotten this far in her career by waffling. Once she made a decision, she stuck to it. And she'd decided on Morgan.

She sipped her beer, then slowly licked the foam from her lips. Morgan's gaze focused on the movement of her tongue. He swallowed hard, and she smiled. Nice to know he was as affected by the attraction between them as she was.

"I don't have my truck here." He shook his head. "Hell, I don't even have a hotel room. I'm staying with a buddy."

"Let me tell you what I have." She took a step closer and ran one neatly polished nail down the pearl snaps of his shirt. "I've got one hour here, then I'm gone. I suggest we make the most of it."

He drew in a breath and let it out slowly, making his chest rise and fall. "Only an hour, huh?" Morgan glanced down at the hand still touching his shirt. He took another gulp of his beer, then lobbed the cup into the trashcan. Taking a step toward her, he closed the distance until they were pressed together. He settled one hand on each side of her waist. "I generally don't like to rush something I enjoy, but in this case I think I can make an exception."

With her heart pounding so hard she was sure he'd hear it, Julia smiled. "Good."

He grabbed her hand. "Let's go."

"Where are we going?" She downed the remainder of the beer and flung the cup into the trashcan as he pulled her after him.

"Someplace I'd wager you've never been in your life." With her hand still captive inside his, Morgan glanced back but didn't stop walking.

His legs were so long Julia struggled to keep up. "That could be anywhere, around this place."

"Yeah, I figured." He laughed as he pushed open an exit door and led her to a parking area behind the building.

Morgan headed down one row of parked horse trailers and cut across to another row before stopping in front of one long, sleek trailer. He dropped her hand, reached beneath the tire and came up with a key.

"What is this?" Julia glanced up at the vehicle, confused to be standing there.

"My buddy's horse trailer." He bounded up two stairs to the door.

Julia remained on the ground, eyeing the trailer with skepticism. "Is the horse inside?"

He paused unlocking the door to look back at her. "Is the city girl afraid of horses?"

"No." Julia frowned. She was all for getting the full cowboy experience, but wasn't sure she could concentrate on what they'd be doing with some huge animal staring.

Morgan flashed his dimples and nodded. "All right, if you say so, but no need to worry. He's still penned inside the arena."

"And your friend?"

"He's still inside too, waiting 'til he can load up his horse. We've got the place to ourselves." Morgan jogged down the stairs to stand on the ground next to her. He ran his fingers down her arms until he reached her hands. "Ready?"

His tone told her *he* was more than ready.

"Definitely." When she nodded, his smile lit the night.

"Good." He led her up the stairs and closed the door behind them. Inside, two narrow beds lined the walls of a living area made for humans, not horses.

Julie glanced around the tight space. "Where does your friend's horse go? In the back?"

"Do you really care?" Morgan stepped close and dipped his head low.

As warmth and anticipation flooded her body, Julia shook

her head. "Not really."

"Didn't think so." He treated her to a slow smile full of promise before he closed the remaining distance between them and touched his lips to hers.

The initial gentleness of his kiss didn't last. Julia tilted her head and parted her lips. Morgan took advantage of her unspoken invitation. With a groan, he tangled one hand in her hair and thrust his tongue against hers.

The stubble on his cheeks and chin that had made him look sexier than hell scratched her face. She didn't care. Pressing closer, she tightened her arms around his back as the tightness inside her body increased.

Morgan walked her backward until her knees hit the edge of the mattress and buckled. She landed on the bed. He gazed down with fire in his eyes.

"I do love a lady in a skirt." Stepping between her legs, he ran his work-roughened hands over her bare thighs, pushing the skirt up to expose her black lace underwear. With eyes heavily lidded with need, he took in the view while dragging in a ragged breath. "Nice panties."

"Nice belt buckle." She gazed past the big, ornate buckle to the long, hard length of him outlined by the denim of his jeans. Swallowing, she realized he'd soon open that belt and give her what she wanted—needed—so badly.

"Thanks, but you don't look like the usual buckle bunny." He smiled slowly, sensually, while he slipped one thick finger beneath the edge of her underwear.

"I don't even know what a buckle bunny is." She let out a soft sigh as his finger slid inside her.

He found her clit with his thumb and pressed against it, making small circles guaranteed to drive her crazy. Her breath quickened, and her muscles bore down, clutching at the finger inside her. Morgan slid in a second one while still working her clit. She let out a low groan.

It had been so long. Too long since she'd had sex, but even longer since she'd been taken by a real man—a man who looked and felt like a man should—big, with rough, strong hands that had never seen a manicure. A man who smelled of good clean sweat mixed with leather and wild animal rather than expensive cologne. He was so strange, so different, so unbelievably tantalizing. Julia nearly laughed as the combination of sensations assaulted her, overwhelmed her.

Her hips rose off the bed. The muscles inside her began to spasm. He bent low and his mouth crashed into hers, muffling her moans of pleasure. She bucked beneath him in time with the thrusting of his hand as the orgasm rocked her. She was still quivering, panting for breath when he stood.

Morgan opened his belt and jeans with a quick, precise dexterity that belied the size of his hands. He reached past her and pawed through a bag on the floor. He rose with a condom packet in his hand and a triumphant smile on his face.

Julia cocked a brow. "I don't know whether to be happy or insulted you're so prepared to bring women here."

He pushed the waistband of his boxer briefs down and the hard length of him sprang forth. Looking at him, she suddenly couldn't care how the condom came to be there, as long as it meant he would be sliding that tempting hard-on into her.

"That's my buddy's bag. The only thing I came prepared to ride tonight was a bull." He grinned and tore into the foil.

"Then I'm very happy he was prepared but you weren't." She ran her tongue over her lips and watched him slide the latex over the impressive erection that would soon be all hers.

"No need to be jealous, sweetheart. Not a woman out there tempted me. That is, until I saw you staring at me."

"I'm not the jealous type." She had been staring. Julia couldn't deny that, but she'd had enough of the chatting. There were better things they could be doing. "Now be quiet and come here."

"My pleasure." He threw his hat onto the other bed and ran one hand through the dark waves of his hair. Then he was between her legs and slipping his hands beneath her hips. He yanked her toward the edge of the mattress, supporting her with his palms.

Still wearing her high heels, she wrapped her legs around his waist.

Pushing her underwear to one side, he poised, ready to enter her. One tilt of his pelvis and he nudged at her entrance. She was so wet, one small push was all it took to have him sliding inside.

Julia forced her eyes open even though the pleasure had them drifting shut. She watched his motions as he pistoned inside her. The same movements and muscle control that she'd seen him use during his ride went to work now to bring her a steadily building pleasure. He loved her until her muscles began to coil tight, ready to release.

The rhythm of his thrusts strengthened the tension inside her until she exploded with another body-wracking climax. As she cried out and pulsed around him, he thrust forward one last time. Holding deep, he came with a shudder and a shout.

Morgan pulled out and collapsed on the bed. She'd just fixed her panties and her skirt when he gathered her into his arms and pulled her close. He traced his fingers down her leg and inched the hem of the skirt she'd just adjusted back up, making small circles on her thigh. "How much time we got left?"

Julia laughed. "I honestly don't know. I kind of lost track."

Morgan turned his head and captured her lips, then trailed

his mouth down her neck to nuzzle the collarbone exposed by her shirt. "Mmm. I'm about ready for round two."

A faint ringing from the bag she'd dumped on the floor told her that wasn't likely to happen. "I need to get that."

With a sigh, he released her. Julia followed the ringing sound and found her phone in the abandoned bag. "Hello?"

"Miss Craven, the tow truck just arrived at your vehicle."

And that was that. Julia glanced at the cowboy stretched on the bed watching her. His buckle and pants still undone. His eyes bright. The color in his cheeks high from the wild ride she was sorry they wouldn't be repeating.

She'd had her fun and two incredible orgasms. No one would know. There'd be no judgment. They'd never see each other again. He didn't even know her last name.

So why did she feel so sad?

Standing on tiptoe, Julia balanced her carry-on over her head, trying to slide it into the bin.

"Need a little help?" The deep and achingly familiar voice sent her heart racing as the weight of the bag disappeared from her hands. She turned and looked up into the face of the man she never thought she'd see again.

Morgan's hat brushed the ceiling of the cabin as he slid his bag next to hers. He grinned. "Fancy seeing you here."

"You're on this flight?" Julia finally found her voice, but it didn't sound like hers. More like a breathy impersonation.

An annoyed huff from behind Morgan had him turning around. "Sorry. Let me get out of your way." He moved out of the aisle; his gaze swung back. "Where are you sitting?"

"Here." She indicated the aisle seat she had yet to take.

The eyes of the woman in the window seat watching the conversation opened wide when Morgan tipped his hat toward her. "Ma'am, I hate to be a bother, but would you mind switching seats with me? Mine's just two rows back."

The flustered woman blushed and couldn't accommodate his request fast enough. Julia had been the subject of his ice-blue stare and sweet-as-honey drawl herself. She knew his power over women well. In fact, by the time she and Morgan were seated side by side, her heart pounded.

"I didn't know you'd be flying today. I mean, what a crazy coincidence."

He shrugged. "Not so much. I live in North Carolina, and this is the only direct flight there today. Where are you headed?"

"I change planes in Charlotte for New York."

"Long layover?" There was a twinkle in his eye that told her he was hoping she'd say yes.

"About an hour." Unfortunately. As her breathing became shallow just from being so close to him, she began to wish she'd miss that connection and be stranded in North Carolina for a while.

"Too bad. You should come back again when you have more time, now you know someone who lives there. There's plenty of room on my ranch for guests."

Julia Craven, city girl, on a ranch. She liked the image. Her cheeks warmed at his invitation, and she wasn't the type to blush. "Maybe I will."

Morgan felt in the breast pocket of his shirt and took out a pen. He scribbled a number on the back of his boarding pass and handed it to her. She took it with a hand she noticed shook a bit.

"Julia, I really enjoyed last night."

She swallowed away her nervousness. "Me too."

"Are you really gonna call or was last night just a one-night thing?"

"I think I'm really going to call." Julia laughed, surprised at her own answer and how good it felt.

"Good." He grinned, and then glanced over his shoulder. "You wanna see if there's enough room in that bathroom for two?"

Her eyes opened wide. "We couldn't."

"Sure we can, darlin'. You only live once. Might as well live dangerously."

Julia laughed. "I guess I should expect a bull rider to say that."

He shrugged, his smile even sexier today than yesterday.

Morgan's gaze dropped to her mouth. He leaned forward, and she knew he was going to kiss her. She also knew she'd been mesmerized by him once again. They'd be in that restroom together, living dangerously, before the flight was over.

When his lips pressed against hers, she figured chances were good she'd be changing her connecting flight home as well. What the hell was it about cowboys? What was it about *this* cowboy? She didn't know, but she was more than willing to spend the time to find out.

DROUGHT

Michael Bracken

Cade Garrett swung off his chocolate-brown quarter horse and stood on the gravel shoulder of the two-lane Farm to Market Road, staring down at me. I'd been sitting in the ditch alongside the road for nearly twenty minutes, nursing a sprained ankle and wondering how I was going to get home. I wore no make-up, my shoulder-length blond hair was pulled back in a loose ponytail, and my sweat-soaked white T-shirt clung to me, clearly revealing the silhouette of my gray sports bra. He slowly took everything in, and then used his index finger to push up the brim of his sweat-stained white Shantung straw Stetson. "Afternoon, ma'am."

"Good afternoon, Mr. Garrett," I replied.

"Seems you've ignored my advice."

A week earlier, when he'd seen me running along the road in front of his ranch, Cade had apprised me of the danger. "Seems I have."

"You take a little tumble, did you?"

"Redneck in a dualie talking on a cell phone ran me off the road," I said. "I don't even think he saw me."

"Can you stand?"

I could and I did, balancing awkwardly on my right foot.

Cade mounted his horse and then reached down and took my arm. In one smooth motion he lifted me into the air and swung me onto the horse behind him. "Wrap your arms around me and hold on tight," he said. "We'll head on up to the house and see what we can do for that ankle."

I did as instructed, flattening my breasts against his broad back as I stretched my arms around his thick chest. I had never ridden a horse before, so rather than moving gracefully with the animal as Cade did, I bounced all around behind him. The friction of my breasts against his back made my nipples stiffen, and I wondered if he could feel them poking him through his blue denim shirt.

We rode along the roadside until we reached the entrance to Cade's ranch, then up the long drive toward his ranch house. Cattle grazed in the pastures on either side of us.

"You have a lot of cows," I said.

"Cattle," Cade corrected, "and not so many." He explained that a drought had affected most of Texas that summer, wreaking havoc on farmers and ranchers. Several small towns, like the one to which I had just moved, had watering bans in place. "It's been so hot and dry this summer," he continued, "that all I'm raising is beef jerky."

I'd had my own drought—more than a year without a sexual encounter of any kind—and his comment made me wonder if I might be drying up and turning into sexual jerky.

At the house, we dismounted and Cade tethered his horse to a porch rail. He helped me up the steps and inside, settling me on a leather couch before disappearing. He returned with a towel, a frozen gel pack, a glass of tap water, and two ibuprofen capsules.

After I washed the capsules down with the tap water, Cade made me lie back on the couch while he shoved a pillow under my calf to prop up my left leg. His hands were warm and rough against my naked calf, and I wished I'd shaved my legs before leaving the house that morning. He loosely wrapped the towel around my swollen ankle and placed the gel pack on top of the towel.

"You just lay there a spell," he said. "I have to take care of Max."

I watched as Cade walked out the front door. I admired the way his faded Wrangler jeans molded so tightly to his backside that I could see his underwear lines. Once he was out of sight tending to his horse, I pushed myself up on one elbow to look around and realized that his living room dwarfed the entire house I was renting just up the road. The furniture was also oversized, with lots of leather and heavy wood, and the room so reeked of testosterone it was obvious that no woman had played a role in decorating it. I smiled, laid back down, and closed my eyes.

I must have fallen asleep waiting for Cade's return, because I opened my eyes to see him sitting in a chair on the other side of the heavy wooden coffee table. He had a magazine open on his lap, but he wasn't reading it. I asked, "Were you watching me?"

"I was wondering if I should change your gel pack again."

"Again?"

"I've changed it twice already."

"How long have I been asleep?"

"Almost two hours."

I sat bolt upright and swung both legs off the couch, sending the gel pack and the towel to the floor. "I'm going to be late."

"For?"

"Orientation," I said. "School starts next week and the new hires are supposed to attend orientation this morning."

"You're a teacher?"

"Not if I miss orientation!" I pushed myself off the couch, put too much weight on my sprained ankle, and promptly fell on my face.

Cade shook his head but didn't rise to help me. "What grade?"

"Third."

He removed a cell phone from his pocket, flipped it open, and dialed.

A moment later someone at the other end answered.

"Billy? I have a Miss—" Cade covered the phone and looked at me. "I never did catch your name."

"Amanda Wilcox."

"—a Miss Wilcox sprawled out on my living room floor and she says—no, nothing like that, you old coot—she says she's supposed to be at orientation this morning and—what?—she was run off the road so I brought her up to the house—and she's going to be a bit late."

After Cade ended the call and returned his cell phone to his pocket, I asked, "Who was that?"

"Your principal."

"You know Mr. Anderson?"

"Billy Bob's my brother-in-law."

"You're married?"

"Nope," he said. "He's my sister's husband."

"Oh."

"He said you ought to get a move on." Cade stood and

stepped around the coffee table. When he held out one hand, I took it. He pulled me to my feet and said, "Wrap your arms around my neck."

I did, and the handsome rancher lifted me into his arms. I'd never known a man strong enough to carry me like that, and I felt a pleasant tingle surge through my body. A bulge in his shirt pocket pressed against my breast, and I shifted position as he carried me out of the house and placed me in the passenger seat of his Ford F-250.

Five minutes later he parked his pickup truck in my driveway behind the seven-year-old Pontiac my father had given me the previous summer and carried me to the porch.

After he set me on my feet, I pointed to my right foot. "My key is down there."

"Under the mat?"

"In a pocket on my shoe," I said.

Cade dropped to one knee and retrieved my key. Then he stood and opened the door. Without waiting for an invitation, he followed me inside.

I turned. "What are you doing?"

"I don't think you'll be able to drive," he said, "so I'll take you to the school."

"It's my left ankle. I drive with my right."

He stared down at me until I relented.

Then Cade sat on my couch, dwarfing it, while I held onto the wall, limped down the hall to my bedroom, grabbed my clothes, and limped back to the bathroom. I showered quickly and didn't realize until I reached for the empty towel rack that all my bath towels were still in the dryer from the previous night.

The washer and dryer were on the little back porch, only accessible through the kitchen, and the route to the kitchen meant crossing the living room in front of Cade, which I wasn't about to do. I opened the bathroom door a crack and called Cade's name.

When he responded, I told him what I needed. He rose from the couch and a moment later stood in the hallway with a bath towel in his hand. I opened the door far enough to stick my arm out.

As Cade handed me the towel, I realized he wasn't looking at me. He was looking past me. "What are you staring at?"

"Your reflection."

I spun around and saw the mirror behind me. Until that moment he'd only been able to see a reflection of my backside. When I realized that by turning I'd just given him the full Monty, I turned red and slammed the bathroom door. Even though I was embarrassed, I was also a little bit excited. I had never flashed anyone before. "You weren't supposed to see me like that!"

After I dried, dressed, and applied the least possible amount of makeup, I limped out of the bathroom. When I reached the living room three steps later, Cade commanded, "Sit."

"Why?"

He pulled an unwrapped Ace bandage from his shirt pocket. "I need to wrap your ankle."

I sat. He wrapped. I had an oversized pair of running shoes—I'd grabbed the wrong box during a going-out-of-business sale and couldn't return them—and I slipped one over the bandage. When we finished I was able to stand a little better than before.

I grabbed my purse and a notebook, and then Cade drove me into town. He pulled into the grade school's parking lot and stopped his pickup truck at the curb nearest the entrance. After shifting the truck into park, he offered to walk me in.

"No, thanks," I told him. "I'll take it from here."

"Call me when you finish, and I'll pick you up." Cade handed me his business card.

"I think I've imposed on you enough," I said. "I'll find my own way home."

"Hardheaded, aren't you?" Cade said. "Good thing you're soft everywhere else."

I ran every day so I *wouldn't* be soft everywhere else. I started to make a smart-mouthed retort but thought better of it. He had, after all, rescued me earlier that morning. I shoved Cade's card in my purse and climbed down from his truck.

"Thank you for your assistance this morning, Mr. Garrett," I said. "If there's ever any way I can repay your kindness—"

"I think your bathroom mirror already did that," he said with a smile that made me suspect he was remembering exactly what he'd seen.

I glared at Cade for a moment. Then I slammed his truck's door and hobbled up the walk to the school. When I stopped at the front door and looked back, Cade touched a finger to the brim of his Stetson and nodded. Then he shifted his truck into gear and drove away.

Although I often thought of Cade—the way his hand felt against my calf when he lifted my leg, the way my breasts felt pressed against his back as we rode his quarter horse up the drive to his ranch house, the way my entire body tingled when he carried me to his truck, the rush of embarrassment tinged with excitement when he'd seen my naked body reflected in my bathroom mirror—I didn't see him again until well after the school year started. By then my ankle had healed, I had found a new, safer route to run each morning, and it still hadn't rained.

I was pushing my cart through the town's only grocery store, dismayed once again at the paltry selection of fresh vegetables and the high prices. It was either that or drive two hours to take advantage of the better shopping opportunities in the nearest small city. When I rounded the corner into the cereal aisle, I almost ran my cart into Cade's jean-clad rear end. He was bent over, retrieving something from the bottom shelf, and his Wrangler jeans were pulled snug across his firm buttocks. I sucked my breath between my teeth and admired the view until he straightened and turned to face me.

A smile split his weathered face in two. He touched the brim of his Stetson and said, "Miss Amanda."

"Mr. Garrett," I acknowledged with a nod. As I spoke I wished I had dressed in something other than a sweat suit before I left the house, and that I had done something with my hair other than pull it back in a ponytail.

"I hear tell you're quite popular with the young'uns."

"And where might you hear that from?"

"Their parents," he said. He nodded toward my ankle. "I see you've healed."

"Yes, I have, thank you," I said. "You had the healing touch."

"So you have no good reason to decline my invitation to the Cattlemen's Ball."

"Excuse me?" I'd lived in town long enough to know that the Cattlemen's Ball was *the* countywide social event, the one evening of the year when the wealthiest ranchers, businesspeople, regional politicians, and anyone else who could scrape together the outrageous admission fee put on their Sunday best and gathered at one of the ranches to hear a fast-rising or slow-fading country music star, dance, gamble, eat, bid on donated goods, and do it all to benefit the county's food pantry.

"I don't have a date," Cade said, "and I have it on good authority that neither do you."

There are no secrets in small towns. "Is this how you usually ask a lady on a date?"

"No, ma'am, it isn't," he said with a sly grin. "I usually wait until they're laid out on the side of the road and can't run away."

"So how long have you been waiting for me to get run off the road again?"

"Nearly a month," Cade said.

"And you felt confident no one else would invite me to the Cattlemen's Ball before you got around to it?"

He answered my question with a question. "Have you been on any dates since you moved to town?"

I shook my head, and the end of my ponytail swept across my shoulders. "I haven't even been asked."

"There's a reason for that," Cade explained. "People saw you riding in my truck. That's as good as wearing my brand."

"*Your brand?*" I stood up straight, my chest rising with indignation.

"You can whoop and holler all you want, but that's just the way things are around here."

"Do you always get what you want?"

"Near enough," he said. "I can't convince God to make it rain and put an end to this drought, but I get pretty much everything else."

"And what makes you think I'll accept your invitation?"

Cade removed his Stetson and leaned close, holding the cowboy hat to prevent others from seeing what passed between us.

"I suspect you want me just as much as I want you," he whispered, his warm breath tickling my ear and sending an erotic tingle through my entire body.

I caught my breath as the heat of desire rushed to my core,

and my nipples dimpled the front of my sweatshirt. I wet my lips with the tip of my tongue and began to breathe again as he pulled away.

I couldn't deny what was so obviously true, and I agreed to accompany Cade to the Cattlemen's Ball.

I was ready before I heard Cade's pickup truck enter the driveway and the engine cut off. When his footsteps crossed the porch, I grabbed my black clutch and opened the door, catching him with one hand upraised to knock.

His eyes opened wide as he drank me in. "You're not wearing that, are you?"

I had chosen a slinky black dress that exposed my décolleté, scooped low in the back, and hugged my curves all the way down to mid-thigh. I'd put my hair up, wore an accenting pearl necklace with matching earrings and new black pumps with two-inch heals that made my legs appear just a little longer and a little firmer than they actually were. "Why not?"

"One look at you dressed like that and all the men will bust their zippers."

I examined Cade from top to bottom. His Stetson was freshly blocked. He wore a crisply pressed blue plaid snap front western shirt, dark blue Wranglers with knife-sharp creases ironed into the legs, a thick leather belt with a dollar-bill-sized buckle holding it in place, and snakeskin cowboy boots.

I had the sinking feeling I should have selected my wardrobe from the feed store, which actually had a large selection of ranch-appropriate western wear, but I said, "I'll take that as a compliment."

"Yes, ma'am," he said. "That was about as good a compliment as I could ever give."

He escorted me to his freshly washed truck, and half an hour later we pulled into the long drive of the Bar-B-Dahl ranch one town south of where we lived. The field to the left of the drive had been designated for parking and was already half-filled with pick-up trucks and SUVs when we arrived.

At the top of the drive, Cade handed his keys to the valet and led me through the hay-bale-lined entrance to the barn where much of the evening's activity would take place. He showed our admission tickets to an older woman with big hair and bigger breasts, and then we were inside.

The dirt-floor barn was as big as an arena football stadium. Gaming tables had been arranged at the near end. At the far corner to the left was a small stage where a local band would play later in the evening, with an open area in front of it for dancing. In the other corner were donated items to be auctioned off. In the middle were several tables arranged in a rectangle where the buffet would be set out, and scattered throughout the barn were several small bars serving beer and wine.

Most of the men were dressed like Cade and so were many of the women, and I quickly learned why cowboy boots were the footwear of choice when we exited the far side of the barn. My heels sank in the soft ground as I struggled to walk across the uneven pasture to where tables had been arranged in front of the outdoor stage. Cade held tight to my elbow to keep me from pitching over.

I overheard two women talking about me as I passed the table where they were seated. One said, "She's not from around here, is she?"

"Not even close," the other replied. "Cade went out and found him a Yankee girl."

As we sat at our table, I saw a fellow teacher—accompanied by the single father of one of my students—several tables away, and I waved to her. She returned my greeting with a wave of her own.

The evening's entertainment was a country star who'd had several hits back in the eighties and nineties, but hadn't charted since the start of the new millennium. He put on a great show, and when it ended we went inside to raid the buffet table. We ate, drank, and gambled with play money until the local band took the stage. Then we danced.

I already knew how to waltz. Cade quickly taught me a basic two-step, and except for the line dances, which we both avoided, we danced away the rest of the evening. He was strong, his movements sure, and he guided me around the dirt floor as if we had been dance partners our entire lives. I was so enamored of Cade that I didn't care I wasn't dressed appropriately and that my expensive heels were dusty by the start of the final dance.

Someone dimmed the barn lights as the band began the only slow song of the evening. Cade pulled me into his strong arms, flattening my breasts against his chest. One big hand on the small of my back pulled me against him, and I quickly realized his belt buckle wasn't the only big thing trapped between us.

I looked up into his eyes, and wet my lips with the tip of my tongue. Cade caught the hint and leaned down until his lips reached mine. We kissed as we danced, oblivious to the fact there were several dozen people on the dance floor with us and several hundred still milling about the barn. By the time the song ended, we weren't actually dancing anymore, just standing in the middle of the dirt dance floor with our tongues in each other's mouths.

When the lights came up, we quickly disengaged. Huskily, Cade said, "I need to get you home."

"The sooner the better," I said, my voice just as thick.

We hurried to the valet stand to wait while a pimple-faced young man found and returned with Cade's truck, and then I pressed myself against Cade during the drive to my house, the palm of my hand resting on his inner thigh, the heel of my hand brushing against the bulge in his Wrangler jeans. We were so focused on one another in the darkness that we didn't notice the storm clouds that had gathered through the night.

We barely made it into the house, the door swinging closed behind us but not quite latching, and then Cade had me in his arms again. He cupped my ass cheeks in his hands and pulled me tight as he buried his tongue in my mouth. Our kiss was hard and deep and took my breath away.

When the kiss finally ended, he pushed me back a step and unfastened the single clasp behind my neck that held up my dress. Fabric slithered down, revealing my unfettered breasts with their constricted areolas and turgid nipples, and then continued past my hips to reveal my red bikini panties. When my dress pooled around my feet, I stepped out of it and toed off my heels.

I stood before him wearing only pearls and panties.

Cade sank to his knees in front of me, hooked his thumbs in the waistband of my panties, and drew them down my thighs until they dropped away on their own. He leaned forward, and his warm breath tickled the closely cropped triangle of blond hair at the juncture of my thighs as he buried his face in my crotch. When he snaked his tongue out and licked my swollen lips, I shifted one foot to spread my thighs and open myself to his oral caresses.

Cade grabbed my buttocks with his big hands, pulled my crotch to his face, and slipped his tongue into my opening. I was hot, wet, and ready, and I moaned with pleasure as he drove his tongue in and out of me. Then he found the tight nub of my clit, sucked it between his lips, and whipped it with his tongue. He licked, he sucked, he licked again, and I began to move my hips forward and back. And then I came hard, banging my pubic bone against his nose as an orgasm swept through me.

My pussy was still clenching and unclenching as Cade stood, spun me around, and bent me over the back of my couch. I heard his zipper slide down, and then the fat head of his cock pressed against my slick pussy lips. He grabbed my hips and drove forward, sinking himself deep inside me. He drew back and pushed forward again and again, his powerful thrusts causing the couch to jump a fraction of an inch across the living room floor each time he slammed into me.

He drove his thick cock faster, harder, deeper, until he drove into me one last time and came with a roar. He leaned against me, trapping me against the back of the couch until he caught his breath and his thick shaft quit spasming.

After Cade pulled away, I made him strip off his clothes, and then I pushed him back on the couch. I bent over him, took his cock in my mouth, and tasted our coupling as I brought it back to life.

Then I straddled Cade and lowered myself onto him. I grabbed his Stetson from the coffee table and plopped it on my head while I rode my handsome, weather-hardened rancher, my tits bouncing this way and that until he reached up and took them in his big hands.

My nipples strained against his palms, my pussy clenched and unclenched around his thick shaft, and I spurred him with my heels as if I were riding his quarter horse. I closed my eyes as I rode him long and hard, and he lasted much longer than he had the first time.

I came, and then I came again, before Cade finally erupted within me. He grabbed my hips and held me still, but he couldn't still my convulsing pussy as it milked his thick shaft.

When I caught my breath, I opened my eyes and looked down at him. He wore the same stupid post-coital facial expression I suspected I wore.

Then I heard something unexpected and looked up. My unlatched front door had swung open. Anyone passing by could have seen what we were doing, and I was glad neither of us had bothered to switch on the lamp. More importantly, though, I could see my front yard and what was causing the noise.

Rain.

Glorious rain.

The drought had ended.

For Texas and for me.

I smiled at the handsome rancher between my thighs. He pulled me down against his chest, knocking his Stetson off my head. We lay together on my couch, watching the storm create mud puddles in my yard, breathing in the fresh scent of rain and the tang of our coupling, and letting our pounding hearts do all the talking.

I couldn't predict the fate of Texas, but I knew then that it would be a long, long time before this transplanted Yankee ever experienced another drought.

ROPED

Charlene Teglia

"If I hear 'Blue Christmas' one more time, I'm going postal."

Regan Morris was too used to talking in court, so she sounded clear and firm and rational when she said it, instead of sounding the way she felt.

She felt like a toddler on the verge of a meltdown, overstimulated by holiday hype and holiday expectations. A small child who lost it at Christmas got a hug. Attorneys were supposed to act like grownups. And she was trying, but inside was a five-year-old who really wanted a hug and no more reminders of how many other people felt blue, too.

"I thought misery loved company," Nancy said. She kept cutting out gingerbread men, unconcerned by Regan's postal potential.

"Misery doesn't want *miserable* company," Regan said, not having to work to match her feelings to her definite tone this time. "Misery would rather be on the other side of the window, where all the happy, pretty people are, instead of stuck out in the cold with the miserable crowd."

"I'm happy. And pretty," Nancy said. Her serene assurance wasn't misplaced. Nancy was gorgeous, even standing in her kitchen in an old pair of Wranglers that had long since frayed at the bottom. The jeans were topped by a stretchy red velvet holiday sweater with fuzzy white trim that should have looked ridiculous, but instead made her look like an elf imported from France to give the North Pole some sophistication. Wisps of dark hair had escaped her sleek updo, but on Nancy, it looked sexy and deliberate instead of messy.

"Of course you are," Regan said, instantly contrite. "Sorry. That's not what I meant."

"I know what you meant." Nancy straightened and set down her cookie cutter. "I know what the problem is. You want to be Cinderella. You want to go to the ball. And instead, you're stuck here with me in the kitchen. It's wrong. You should go to the ball."

"Was there a lot of rum in the rum balls?" Regan asked.

"Yes, but that isn't the point." Nancy was focused on something other than pastry now, and from long experience Regan knew that didn't bode well. Whatever Nancy focused on got done. "You're blue because you're single and it's the holidays, and staying with me and my husband and our two-point-five kids isn't helping. So your fairy godmother is going to send you to the ball."

Regan was fairly sure even Nancy couldn't produce a formal dance in the wilds of Wyoming, so she helped herself to another treat. "I'm testing these for quality assurance," she murmured. And also for possible anesthetic properties.

"Better make that your last." Nancy finished the tray of gingerbread men with speed and precision, popped them into the oven, and set the timer. "I can get you dressed and lend you a coach, but you'll have to drive yourself."

Regan laughed.

"No, really. There's a big party at one of the neighboring ranches. I'll tell them you're coming. One more guest won't be a problem. There are never enough single women out here. You can take the Caddy; I never use it."

The Cadillac was a gas-guzzling monster. It was also not built for navigating gravel roads, let alone icy, snow-covered gravel roads. "I'm starting to think you're serious about this."

"I am. Remember when you didn't go to the senior prom? You were too busy studying and working at your part-time job, saving for college. I didn't know how to be a fairy godmother then, so I'm making up for it now."

Regan's jaw dropped. "The prom? You think my adult life was in any way affected by not going to the prom?"

"Maybe. I went; you didn't. We had different priorities. Your priorities aren't making you very happy right now, so why not change them?" Nancy dragged her into the walk-in master closet and started rummaging through garment bags. "No. No. Maybe. No...oh, *yes*."

Regan peered at the chosen dress through the clear plastic cover. "No."

"Trust me." Nancy freed the dress and shook it out. About a million miles of green taffeta filled the space between them. "It's one of those dresses you have to see worn to get the effect."

"It looks like a prom dress," Regan pointed out.

"It's Dior. From my modeling days. You couldn't afford this for prom."

"I couldn't afford it now." Regan took the dress gingerly. "I have law school debt on top of college debt. Plus a mortgage. I don't buy Dior gowns."

"Which is why you need a fairy godmother. Look, matching

shoes!" Nancy fished one out of the bottom of the garment bag and waved it in triumph.

"I'll never be able to walk in those," Regan said.

"They're not for walking. They're for dancing. Let some hot cowboy help you balance, and you'll be fine. Come on, get changed."

Two hours later, Regan decided Nancy's plan had merit. The shoes were going to cripple her if she didn't get them off by midnight, but the cowboy two-stepping her cheerfully toward the mistletoe was happy to keep her upright. And since he was used to wrestling steers, a too-thin, overworked attorney wasn't going to strain his muscles.

"My turn," a low voice said in her ear as a hand reached from behind her to tap her partner.

The voice was familiar. Regan froze as a man stepped into view. A man forever burned into her memory—one she hadn't expected to see here, now. He was older, harder, with a mouth that looked like it had forgotten how to smile, a face framed by black hair in need of a trim and dominated by eyes that resembled a winter sky with a storm approaching.

Travis or Tate or whatever his name was surrendered her with the same cheer he'd tried to seduce her with and moved on to the next possibility. The man who replaced him wasn't going to go away nearly as easily.

"Regan."

"Jonas."

They began to dance. Regan had no idea what to say. It took all her concentration not to lose an ankle to the shoes while the man who was damn well not Prince Charming held her close and led her around the room with practiced ease.

When the silence got to her, she broke it with, "It's been a long time."

"Has it? Seems like yesterday I woke up in that hotel room with no idea if I was going to be a father at eighteen, or if I'd ever hear from you again if I was."

Regan stumbled. "Damn these shoes."

"I hope they hurt."

That was a bit much. Regan pulled herself together, which was difficult to do with one shoe half off. The Dior helped her dignity. She hoped. "This is not the place for this conversation."

The gathering storm lit wintry blue eyes. "You're so right." Without another word, he swept her off her feet and carried her away from the safety of the crowd.

"Where are you taking me?" Regan asked, trying to sound unconcerned. She debated stopping him, but really, if he was determined to make a scene, it was better to do it in private, and it wasn't like he was going to hurt her. Embarrass her, disturb her, maybe. Hurting a woman, however, wasn't in Jonas's repertoire.

She felt less certain on that point when he didn't answer. Even less sure when he shut her in a distant bedroom, produced a length of rope from the closet, and set her on the bed.

"Whoa, cowboy." Regan started to roll away, but he caught her in a firm grip and started winding rope around her wrists with a speed that proved he deserved all his calf-roping wins. "Bondage? Really? What happened to *hello?*"

"Hello, Regan." Jonas continued his work without pausing, making knots and securing the rope to the headboard. "This is my way of making sure you don't run off before I'm finished with you."

"I didn't run off the last time," Regan said, exasperated. "You're a heavy sleeper."

"Not that heavy." Jonas took her shoes and, after a quick

glance around the room, opened the window and threw them into a snowbank.

"Hey!"

"Can't run off in the snow barefoot," Jonas said, crossing muscular arms over his broad chest as he stared down at her.

"Those weren't mine," Regan moaned. "They were Nancy's. They didn't come from Payless."

"Nancy? That friend of yours who went off to become a supermodel before marrying the cowboy next door?"

"Yes."

"She won't miss them."

That was probably true. Regan switched to a topic that might actually get her somewhere. "What are you doing here, Jonas?"

"It's my ranch." He didn't miss the surprise in her eyes. "Nancy didn't tell you?"

"No." Regan had assumed he'd left forever when he'd gone away to achieve whatever it was the town bad boy was destined for. The vague vision made her realize she hadn't thought much about an adult Jonas; he'd stayed eighteen in her memory, the dangerous boy all the girls wanted, an impossible dream for a bookish, flat-chested girl.

Her impossible dream continued to stare down at her, but Regan was used to courtroom tactics and refused to let it intimidate her. She attempted to settle into a comfortable position, although her bound wrists didn't allow much room to maneuver. "Okay. You wanted to talk. Talk."

"Am I a father, Regan?"

That was straight to the point. "No. I was on the pill."

"You were a virgin."

Like it had somehow slipped her mind. "Thank you," Regan said, her voice as dry as the winter air. "I went on the pill at sixteen anyway. Fifty percent of pregnancies in this country are unplanned. I didn't want to become a statistic."

He continued to stare, and she knew the picture she made in the dress, sprawled across the mattress in a cloud of green fabric that brought out the green flecks in her brown eyes and created the illusion of cleavage.

"You didn't become a statistic."

"No. Is that all?"

He scowled at her. "Christ, Regan. I knew you your whole life. One day you suddenly decide to ride me like a wild bull, the next you disappear."

"I didn't disappear. I went to school. You went off on the rodeo rounds." And they hadn't exactly known each other. Known *of* each other, yes. But they'd been from different worlds, and she'd understood that perfectly well.

"You didn't tell me where. You didn't leave a number. Nancy was never in the same country for more than five minutes so I couldn't ask her."

Regan's brows rose. "You wanted to know where I was?"

"Yes, I wanted," Jonas growled. His eyes took on a different gleam. "I still want." He started toward her.

"I thought you wanted to talk," Regan reminded him warily. Talking she could cope with.

"Talking is overrated."

When his lips found hers, Regan decided it was a valid point. Why waste lips like those on anything but tasting, testing, sinking into them with all her pent-up frustration and dissatisfaction?

So she did, and he kissed her back with all the heated frenzy she remembered from that long-ago night when she'd thrown caution to the wind and given herself one unforgettable going-away present.

There was a difference, though, the evidence of time and experience tempering the kiss into something stronger, bolder, and more seductive than memory.

She laughed a little against his mouth.

He pulled back. "What?"

"You've gotten better at this."

"So have you." By his narrowed eyes and the deepening tone of his voice, that didn't seem to be a happy thought for him.

Irrationally, that pleased her. "Let's see what else you're better at." She waved her bound hands, then stretched them above her head. "I'm at your mercy."

"I don't have any." Jonas set out to prove his words with action, kissing her into mindless heat before nipping her lower lip, grazing the curve of her neck with the edge of his teeth, and lifting her enough to undo the zipper holding up the dress so the sleeveless bodice slid away without resistance. Cool air tightened her bared nipples into stiff peaks before Jonas covered one with the rough palm of his hand and the other with his wicked mouth.

Regan let out a choked moan as he used hands, mouth, and teeth to send enough heat rippling through her body to melt the snow outside. She arched up, trying to get more of his exquisite torture, while longing for those hands to move under her skirt and between her legs where she could feel herself growing slick and ready. But she couldn't use her hands to urge his down, and the knowledge that she really was at his mercy created an erotic tension that heightened every touch, every kiss.

Jonas raised his head and moved back to push the yards of fabric up to her waist so she was bare above and below it, except for the scrap of a thong she wore. He hooked his fingers into it and tore it away, then looked down at her, a half smile turning up one corner of his mouth. "Why, Regan, you wax now."

Unreasonably, that made her blush. "Everybody does," she mumbled.

"Not everybody gets the full Brazilian."

She narrowed her eyes at him. "No? Then how do you know what it's called?"

"You said it yourself—I've gotten better at this. I haven't spent the past ten years living like a monk." He tilted his head to one side just a bit, considering her. "I wonder if I remembered to lock the door."

Jonas stood, but instead of checking, he unbuttoned, unzipped, and tugged his jeans down to his thighs. Regan's eyes went to the cock that rose up to his navel, fully erect. It seemed even larger than she'd remembered. She felt a greedy thrill, wanting all of the breadth and length of him filling her empty, aching sheath.

When he knelt between her open legs and started lowering himself down, Regan remembered herself. "The door."

"What of it?" He kissed her belly, licked her navel, then kissed the soft, bare skin just above her clit.

"You weren't sure you locked it." Her voice came out a little breathless as she waited, torn between wanting his mouth to move lower right now and making sure he wouldn't be interrupted once it did.

"That's right." He licked at her, a long and lazy caress, just tasting before raising his head to look into her eyes. "Somebody might walk in and see you all exposed, tied up, with me between your legs."

Her breath froze in her chest as his words hit home.

"Too much for you? Tell me to stop."

Regan briefly weighed the risk versus the overpowering need burning through her. If they stopped now, the moment would be lost, and she didn't think it would come again. "Don't stop.

Unless—dammit, do you have a condom?"

"Didn't come prepared?" Jonas licked at her again as if savoring a forbidden treat.

"Not for this."

"I did." The assurance left her torn between relief and agonizing suspense. He fastened his mouth over her clitoris and suckled while his tongue did swirls and flicks that had her hips bucking. It was amazing, but not enough. When he thrust two fingers into her, it was all she needed to go over the edge, the orgasm hitting her like a sucker-punch and leaving her limp and breathless.

"Like that?" He sounded smug, but under the circumstances, maybe he was entitled.

"Um," Regan murmured assent.

"You'll like this better." Jonas gave her a knowing look as he produced a condom and rolled it down the length of his shaft before closing his fist around the base and guiding the head of his cock to her opening.

"All I Want for Christmas Is You" played in the distance, a reminder of the party going on beyond the bedroom, and Regan realized this was exactly what her dissatisfaction had called for. Jonas, hard and hot, over her, in her.

He thrust home, and the past and present blurred with one constant linking them: she wanted him. Wanted this. It was crazy to give her virginity to a wild rodeo hero; equally crazy to do this, now, with a house full of guests. And she didn't care. She hadn't cared then. She didn't care now.

"God, yes," she groaned as he began to move. His mouth claimed hers again, and she tasted herself on him. Her inner muscles clenched around the width of his cock as he pressed deep, pulled back, then drove deeper. She rocked with him, taking everything he gave her, reaching for more.

His hands moved under her, cupping her ass and holding her where he wanted her while he fucked them both into oblivion, and she felt his cock throb as he released with a rough groan. Then he sprawled over her while galloping heartbeats slowed and their lungs caught up with their ragged breaths.

He levered himself up and gave her a hard, brief kiss. "Be right back."

She had a second to blink in disbelief that he was leaving her here, like this, before she realized he was just crossing the room to toss the spent condom in the wastebasket. He turned back to her, his gaze moving over her body as he tucked his still half-erect penis into boxers and pulled his jeans back into position, snapping and zipping until no physical sign of what he'd been doing remained.

"Jonas?" She tugged at the rope as a reminder.

"Oh, no." He returned to sit on the bed beside her, one hand trailing up and down her bare leg. "I'm not letting you go just yet. I want to know something first."

"What?"

Jonas cupped his hand over her hairless, glistening mound. "Why me?"

"Then or now?"

"Both. But start with then. You weren't some buckle bunny looking for a quick ride."

"Had a few of those, have you?"

"Yes, and you're not answering me."

Regan blew out a breath. "Because I wanted you."

"To be your first?" He gave her an unreadable look. "It never made any sense. You weren't the type to have casual sex with a guy you weren't even dating."

She paused for a moment, mentally replaying a few highlights. "I don't think it was all that casual. I remember wondering if the police were going to be called. We weren't very quiet, and that was before we tore the shower curtain and broke the bed."

"It was a lot of things, but casual wasn't on the list," Jonas agreed. "I paid the damages, and it was worth every penny. When I couldn't find you, I used to throw darts at the bill, cursing your name."

"I wasn't exactly hiding," Regan said. She left the rest alone, afraid to think about what it meant.

"You made it clear you didn't want me to find you. You took what you wanted and took off. And every time I had a lover, for an hour or a week, I had that to compare it to. The world is full of women, Regan, but only one of them is you."

Oh. Yes. That. "I found it generally more satisfying to masturbate," she admitted.

He closed his eyes and shook his head, looking almost pained. "Christ, the things you say and do. I don't expect it, you look so cool and controlled, like rolling around with a sweaty cowboy would make you curl your lip, and then you goad me to go to my limit."

"Do you have limits?"

"Yes." He took his hand away, leaving her exposed and bereft of his touch. "Here's one; I don't want casual. I don't want one hot fuck before you leave me in the cold and go back to wherever you flew in from."

"Boston," she volunteered. "And if you think it's cold here, try it some time."

"If you're there, I'll do it."

Her breath stopped.

"Say something," he ground out, almost glaring at her.

Her mouth opened, closed, before she finally managed to say, "You'll do what?"

"Try it. Boston. You and me."

"You have a ranch to run," she pointed out.

"And you have a career. Those are details. I'm not saying long distance is going to work forever, but I want to find out if *we* do."

"If we what?" Regan asked stupidly.

"Work forever." He gave her a challenging look. "You up for it?"

She felt a silly smile breaking over her face. "I'm up for anything you dish out."

They never made it back to the party. Regan was pretty sure her fairy godmother wasn't surprised when she didn't make it back before midnight, either.

ROUGH STOCK

M. Marie

Next up, Kennedy Rawlings!"

Dawson Conway squinted against the bright, midday sun and looked toward the ring as the announcer called out the name of the next competitor. Across the dusty showground, he picked out his boss and Mrs. Rawlings from the crowd. The middle-aged couple stood close together near the bucking chute.

Even from this distance, the young ranch hand could see the unease and worry in their faces and frames. Jake Rawlings stood tall and stiff. It was rare to be at an outdoor event in their small town and not hear his pleasant laughter spreading infectiously through the crowd, but today he stood silent, without a hint of a smile. His eyes stared out at the quickly clearing ring, but Dawson knew the only thing he really saw was the chaos and confusion of last year's train wreck.

Beside Mr. Rawlings, his wife watched nervously as the pickup team helped the previous round's unsuccessful rider from the ring. Her left hand was clenched tightly in the extra fabric of her denim skirt, while her right hand gripped her husband's forearm. Molly Rawlings was a sturdy, strong woman, but today, as she clung to her partner for support, she looked fragile and vulnerable.

In all his years working on the Rawlings' ranch, Dawson had only seen her look this way once before; recalling the shock of her unexpected weakness that day, and the heavy fear it had spread through his own body, he looked away quickly.

It wouldn't do his nerves any good to remember something like that today.

Instead, he focused on the rest of the audience. Word had spread through their small Alberta town that Kennedy would be competing in the women's rodeo again this year, and the rumors had certainly drawn a crowd.

Normally, the women's events didn't draw half the spectators that the professional rodeos did, but today the fairground was packed. Dawson wished he could believe it was all in support of her—and certainly a number of the onlookers were there for exactly that reason—but he could tell from the hushed whispers following her name and the excited ripple spreading through the crowd that the majority of the spectators had only come in the hopes of seeing another disaster.

To keep from showing his anger, in case the Rawlings or one of their sponsors spotted him, Dawson pulled his worn-out Resistol down over his eyes and crossed his arms. For the big rodeos, the ranch usually hired him as a pick-up man riding a good-natured mare, but they never asked it of him for the women's rodeos, and he never offered. With his jacket collar turned up and his hat pulled down low, he simply stood by the southwest corner of the paddock like a sentinel on guard, watching, waiting, and worrying.

A sudden hush, then a flurry of excited whispers heralded her approach. Flicking the brim of his hat up, Dawson glanced back across the showground as Kennedy advanced. Like all the Rawlings, she was impossible to mistake, even in a crowd. That family carried their personalities in their gaits, and Kennedy's stride spoke of confidence, fearlessness, and a fierce, indomitable pride.

He grinned openly as she boldly cut her way through the crowd. Her shoulders were rolled back, her chin was thrust out, and her hips swaggered like a true *vaquera*.

At nineteen, Kennedy had finally grown into the long-legged, awkward body she had been teased for all through school. She was a tough, tall girl with a solid, athletic build. Like the champion stock her father bred, she was broad-shouldered and muscular. Rough-mannered and rough-spoken, she had a reputation for always speaking her mind. She could be quick-tempered at times, and although she was by no means reckless, she had a fiercely stubborn, competitive side. Like her father, when she set a challenge for herself, she would push herself to her absolute limit to reach her goal.

It was a trait that had brought Jake Rawlings his early success as a young man working the circuits, and had become the driving force behind Kennedy's decision to carry on the family tradition by competing in rodeos as well.

Her career choice wasn't unusual for their community. Their town always had a strong showing of participants in the women's rodeo, and a handful of local girls also competed in the professional circuit. Kennedy's family certainly would have supported her if she had shown an interest in following a similar professional path, but she'd bristled at the idea. The pro competitions were too restrictive; women could only compete in a handful of events, the bulk of which were timed ones.

Although Kennedy was a natural at barrel racing and team roping, her heart wasn't in it.

She lived for the rough stock events; she thrived on the risk and danger of testing herself physically against the raw power and strength of the broncos and bulls.

All this gave Kennedy a reputation for being wild and fearless. Even her parents held that opinion of her, but Dawson knew better. She wasn't as thick-skinned as she let on.

Dawson's mind strayed to the night before. He had just finished checking over the stock at the end of his shift and was about to make his way back toward the main house when a shadow fell across his path.

Kennedy leaned against the side of the barn a few meters ahead, unsmiling.

He paid no mind to her unpleasant expression. The fact she'd waited outside the barn so long her impatient pacing had worn a noticeable furrow in the dirt spoke more clearly to her current mood than her forced scowl did. She was desperate to see him.

Dawson felt his lips curl up affectionately at her contrariness. He had known her for years—the six years he'd worked on her family's ranch and a full decade of school before that. They'd grown up together.

Even as a child, she'd hidden her emotions behind a mean look, but he'd never been put off in the least by her posturing. In all honesty, it was what had first drawn him to her. He'd always wanted to see what type of girl hid behind all those harsh glares and curt words.

He flashed her a cheerful smile and tipped his worn hat in her direction. "Evening, Miss Rawlings."

In the low light, he saw her roll her eyes, but also smile faintly. "Shut up, Dawson," she snorted, as she shouldered past and slunk into the barn.

The amused ranch hand turned and followed, too curious about her presence to leave, even though he knew his weekly paycheck and a hot dinner were both waiting for him up at the house.

Pulling the barn door shut behind him, he watched her. She seemed restless and agitated. Her shoulders were tense under her thin flannel shirt, and she carried her Stetson in her left hand, slapping it against her thigh with every second step, distractedly. She wandered past each animal's stall, but seemed completely oblivious to the lifted heads and soft whickers of greeting.

He quietly trailed behind her, petting each animal he passed soothingly. He was beginning to worry. Kennedy was usually tirelessly devoted to the animals, particularly the horses. As she disappeared into the tack room, he hurried after her.

At the small room's threshold he paused and watched her pace to the end of the room, then stop and stare blankly at the row of harnesses.

"Are you looking for something?" he asked.

She glanced over her shoulder and met his concerned gaze, but didn't reply.

They stared at each other for a long moment before Dawson risked a more personal guess. "Do you want to talk about tomorrow?"

Kennedy's eyes finally came alive. "There's nothing to talk about. I'm fine!" she snapped, visibly stiffening.

So that's what was bothering her. Dawson took an apologetic step back, and raised his hands in surrender. "Sorry, Ken. No harm meant. Just trying to be helpful."

"I don't need any help," she said, her voice gruff.

He nodded and leaned against the doorframe. "'Course not. You're practically a pro."

She answered his teasing with another derisive snort, but this time there was less anger behind her gaze as she looked at him.

He knew where her mind was wandering. Last year's fall had shocked them all, but none more so than Kennedy herself. She had come out of the bucking chute sitting strong and tall on the bronco. As soon as she marked the horse out, she gripped her thighs tight and began to count down the eight seconds. The horse's first jump didn't stir her in the least, and a confident grin had spread over her face—but that was short-lived.

With his second buck, the horse shook her loose. She lost her grip on the rigging and instinctively reached down with her free hand to try to grab her mount's mane. She knew she was disqualifying herself with the action, but even that illegal move wasn't enough to restore her balance. With his next powerful kick, the bronco threw her off.

She landed hard.

The pick-up men had all rushed into the ring. The obnoxious, efficient rodeo clown distracted the agitated horse before it could trample her. He lured the gelded male to the pipe, where he was calmed and quickly herded back into the bucking chute. On the other side of the ring, the attending medic knelt in the dirt beside Kennedy's prone form.

As the Rawlings rushed through the gate and across the dirt toward him, Dawson suppressed a sinking heart and rose, wiping his sweaty hands on his pants, and began the unenviable task of trying to reassure them as they waited for the ambulance to arrive.

Kennedy woke up in the hospital two days later with a concussion, a broken arm, and a handful of fractured ribs. Under her mother's anxious eye, she had slowly healed over the next few months.

Knowing she was too competitive and determined to quit with such a tarnished performance record, her father had reluctantly helped her back into the saddle as soon as she was physically able, and her training had resumed.

Now, a year later, she was fit and capable of competing again, but her confidence was still injured from the incident. With her return to the rodeo less than twenty-four hours away, he could see that she struggled with self-doubt and anxiety.

In the soft voice he used to coax and calm skittish horses, he whispered, "I just want to help, Kennie."

Dropping her gaze to her scuffed working boots, she sighed. "I just need to get my mind off of last time," she admitted quietly. "I need a distraction."

Looking back up, she caught his eye and gave him a deadpan, serious look. "Do you really want to help to me, Dawson?"

A loud cheer from the crowd pulled Dawson's mind back to the present. He looked over to the pipe just in time to see the gate open and Kennedy explode out of the bucking chute in a blur of straining muscles, whipping hair, and stomping hooves. Every gaze was on her as her round began.

As a concession to her anxious parents, she wasn't riding bareback this year. She was balanced atop a specialized saddle and gripped the simple rein tightly. Her free hand reached up to the sky above her.

As her mount reared up for his first jump, she marked the horse, gripped down hard with her legs, and braced herself.

Watching her jaw clench as she struggled to balance herself despite the horse's irregular rhythm, Dawson remembered how she had tightened her jaw last night as well after he had confirmed his desire to help her in any way he could.

Her face had been a hard mask as she stared him down, trying to judge the sincerity of his offer before finally nodding and stepping closer. "Then take off your shirt," she demanded.

When Dawson didn't immediately reach up and begin to

undo his buttons, Kennedy impatiently grabbed him by the front of his work shirt and pulled him into the room. Ignoring his weak protests, she pushed his back against the closest wall and pressed up against him.

Unlike the other girls who had propositioned him in the past, Kennedy's body was hard and firm as she pressed it against his. She also didn't waste any time on sweet words or false promises.

Her rough hands moved firmly to his waist and pulled his shirt out of his pants. Once the fabric was free, she hastily yanked it up over his head.

Momentarily blinded, he cursed, then startled to hear a bark of laughter from Kennedy. Eagerly pulling his shirt off, he looked at her, but his teasing smile fell into an open-mouthed gasp as he spotted her.

With her hands on her hips and an unflinchingly serious expression on her face, she stared back at him, topless. Her shirt was crumpled on the ground between them.

His first thought had been shock at how pale her skin was underneath her t-shirt. The difference in pigments marked by the distinct tan lines around her neck and upper arms fascinated him. Letting his eyes travel over the paler terrain, he took in her small but firm breasts and her muscular waist. His eyes lingered there a moment, until he noticed the silence had stretched out too long.

Glancing up, he met her narrowed gaze. There was something harsh and challenging in her stare, but the way her arms slowly rose to cross over her chest spoke of a mounting vulnerability as well.

Dawson knew he had to speak carefully to relieve her unease, and sugary compliments wouldn't work on this breed of girl.

Smiling roguishly, he nodded toward her bared skin. "Cute freckles," he teased.

The tension broke. "Shut up!" she snapped, but her eyes were bright as she shoved him to the ground.

There was a sharp inhale of breath throughout the crowd as the bronco bucked violently. Pulled out of his thoughts, Dawson looked to the ring in alarm, but Kennedy held on. She was determined to finish her ride today, just as she had been determined to do the same last night.

She had reached for her belt buckle, and he had hastily done the same. Kicking off his boots and jeans, he had just managed to bare himself when she dropped onto the ground beside him. They were both already breathing hard as she climbed on top of him and spread her legs.

Without any preamble, Kennedy had then reached down between their bodies and with one rough hand, gripped him tightly to guide his cock inside her opening.

Watching her ride now, Dawson's mind relived their encounter the night before. As the jumping bronco came down hard on the ground, he remembered his exhilaration as she pushed him down onto the pile of spare horse blankets.

As her legs tightened around her bucking mount, his abdomen ached where her strong thighs had gripped him as she straddled him. The chain around his neck had been her rein as she used her hips and legs to set their rhythm.

It had been a uniquely gratifying experience. Her vagina was tight and hot, but it wasn't very wet, despite her aggressive interest in their encounter. Her cunt gripped him roughly as he thrust up into her, and the limited lubrication increased the friction to the very edge between pleasure and pain.

She smelled of sweat, rope, and horses. Her body was hard, her hands calloused.

When he reached up and squeezed her breasts, she didn't gasp or moan as his previous girlfriends had. She cursed obscenely, lips pulled back in a feral smile, and slammed her hips down, grinding hard against him.

He groaned loudly as she mimicked her countless bronco rides, bucking up and down on his hard shaft. Her grip was bruising, and her eyes burned with need. Her tight pussy squeezed him, but gradually moistened; her movements grew more fluid.

Gripping her hips to help her find a less jarring rhythm, he let her sate herself on his cock, more than content to have her use him while he watched her small breasts shiver, the tight, pink nipples too tempting to ignore.

He plucked them with one hand, ignoring the tightening of her jaw and the resumed frenzy of her crashing hips. A light sheen of sweat coated both their bodies. Their breath grew more labored. And then she raised one hand, her back arched, and her movements slowed to a rolling gait as whimpers seeped from her mouth. Her eyes closed, and she appeared lost inside herself.

He'd watched, transfixed, as all her hard edges seemed to melt away with the pleasure causing the sweet convulsions rolling through her hot walls.

He hadn't dared to embrace her, but he'd been satisfied knowing her stress and worry were exhausted away long before they reached a mutual climax. When Kennedy and Dawson did both finally orgasm, they sagged down onto the itchy, coarse blankets, trembling from the exertion and exposed emotions.

Rolling over, Dawson stared into her eyes. She was too tired for pretenses and looked back at him honestly. The raw emotions cut right to his core: fear, anxiety...desire.

Reaching out, he took her hand and squeezed it. "I love you, Kennedy."

Rolling her eyes, she stretched out on her back and folded

her arms under her head. "I don't want to hear that right now. I just want to relax."

"What about tomorrow then?" he teased, biting at her earlobe.

Growling, she had rolled over and pinned him again, sliding her hips over his, then coming down to kiss him—not a tender gesture, but a fierce, hot brand. When she lifted her head, her lips turned up in a confident smirk as she promised, "When I win, then you can tell me."

Watching her now as the final seconds of her round ticked down, he let himself relax. There was such a sharp contrast between the stiff tension and nervous energy that had plagued her the night before and her condition today. She was in the perfect shape to ride; her body was loose, her mind focused, and, regardless of the outcome, her confidence and pride would be restored by her bold performance.

Dawson grinned and began to make his way toward the nearest gate as the crowd began to cheer wildly. He didn't need to hear the announcer's declaration to know who had finally won.

THE RANCH HAND

Sedona Fox

The Solt Ranch was a prime piece of Montana real estate. With his health declining as it was, and no sons to take over the cattle business, John Solt all but jumped at the offer presented to him in a letter from a wealthy businessman in Nevada. Forsythe had made his fortune in the California gold rush and was looking for a more sustainable investment. Like any good investor, Forsythe knew that gold veins could run out at any time, but raising cattle would last for generations. John's only obstacle was his daughter. Headstrong and independent, she wanted nothing to do with the offer.

"Papa, this is our place! You can't mean to sell it," Charlene said, anger stiffening her spine. "I can run it just fine on my own, if you'd just give me half a chance."

"It's not a woman's place to control the operations of a ranch," John said. "It takes a man's business sense to keep the respect of his employees. Besides, it wouldn't be a sale outright. The future of our land depends on you, Charlene."

Something in his tone made her eyes narrow in suspicion. "What's that supposed to mean?"

Her father cleared his throat, and she saw his dread as he revealed the second part of the offer. "Forsythe is sending a ranch hand ahead of him to determine the worth of the land and of...you," he said gently. "He wants your hand in marriage. He wishes to settle down and believes that a union with you will help in the transition of ownership with the workers."

Charlene's furious eyes burned with unshed tears. "So I'm just another business transaction? Something to be sold like a head of cattle? How can you even consider such a thing? I thought you cared about me."

"Charlene, my love for you is why I am considering his proposal. I want to be sure you're taken care of when I pass. His man is arriving tomorrow, and I expect you to be on your best behavior while he's here. And please, start wearing something feminine. I can't have you traipsing around in pants and boots, pretending you're one of my employees."

"Papa! How can you do this to me?" She tried to hold the tears back. "I don't want to marry some fat, pompous businessman. He's probably old, and hideously ugly too. Why else would he send such a ridiculous offer through the mail?"

"Please do this for me." John spoke with a dejected voice. "You don't know that Forsythe is all of those things. He could be perfect for you."

She sighed as a single tear escaped. "Only for you, Papa."

Charlene escaped to her room and quietly broke down as she rummaged through the cedar chest at the foot of her bed for something her father would consider appropriate. After choosing a deep blue dress, she laid out the undergarments she would be forced to endure the next day: corset, underskirts, and stockings. She hated each item. They constricted her and made her look fragile. Once she had bathed and dressed for bed, she braided her long brown hair and stared at her reflection in the mirror.

Charlene had thought that, at barely twenty, she still had time to enjoy her youth. But no longer. Now she would be judged according to her worth as the possession of a man she had never seen.

After a restless night, Charlene dressed and met her father for breakfast. She had taken great care with her appearance to please him, even arranging her hair into a loose bun at the crown of her head and held in place with a carved bone comb. As for the ranch hand and his employer, she couldn't care less what they thought of her. She was already planning to sneak away at every opportunity to perform her usual ranch chores. If the new ranch hand caught her in the act, all the better.

Then perhaps he would take word back to Forsythe that the woman he sought was uncontrollable and boyish. As it was, she felt short of breath from the corset and was unable to eat much. She wanted nothing more than to take a pair of shears to the torturous garment.

"You look beautiful this morning," John said, smiling his approval. "Thank you. I know how much you detest wearing such things."

"Only for you, Papa," she muttered once more, not daring to look at his face for fear she would burst into tears again.

The arrival of Forsythe's man caused a stir among the workers as he rode past the corrals. John and Charlene stood on the porch awaiting his arrival, the rattling of Charlene's nerves adding to the suffocation of her clothing. As he approached, she could see that his horse carried not only its rider, but several dusty saddlebags and a coiled rope hanging down the right flank. The rider himself was attired in well-worn leather chaps covering his denims, a light brown bib shirt, and a darker brown oilskin coat. His tan pinchfront cowboy hat shadowed his eyes and obscured his expression.

He brought the steed to a halt, dismounted, and walked up the steps to greet her father. Charlene took in the sight of him: a regular ranch hand type. When he removed his leather gloves, she saw calluses on his palms—this man worked hard. The muscular build that filled out his clothing also spoke to years of hard labor. What astonished Charlene, though, was his height. Her father was taller than most at five foot ten, but this man made him look small—he was at least six foot three.

Removing his hat and stuffing the gloves inside, he held out a hand to John. "Morning, Mr. Solt. Name's Jesse Broadwell, Mr. Forsythe's head ranch hand."

His deep voice had a slight drawl, and its timbre sent a strange chill down Charlene's spine.

"Morning, Mr. Broadwell. This is my daughter, Charlene."

Turning to face her, the ranch hand showed her the most disarming smile. "Ma'am," he said with a nod. "Please, you can both just call me Jesse."

He hadn't looked away from her as he spoke the last part, and Charlene couldn't help but stare. Deep down she knew it was rude, but she couldn't help herself. Jesse's blonde hair was just long enough that it fell into his startling blue eyes. His skin was a golden tan, and his smile revealed the most charming laugh lines she had ever seen. The stubble on his face gave him a rugged appearance, but it didn't take away from his youthful looks. She would have guessed he couldn't be more than twenty-eight.

"Would you care for some breakfast, Jesse?" John asked, apparently oblivious to Charlene's lack of manners.

Jesse finally broke their gaze and looked back to the man

addressing him. "If it's all the same to you, sir, I'd like to start familiarizing myself with the operations here. Mr. Forsythe will arrive in a week's time wanting a full report, so it's best I begin as soon as possible."

"Of course," John said with a smile. But Charlene could hear a hint of sadness. Only one week and the fate of his ranch and his daughter's future would be decided.

John and Charlene, along with some of the senior ranch hands, spent the morning giving Jesse a tour of the ranch. Charlene stole glances when she was certain he wasn't looking. But he caught her a time or two, and she would have sworn he'd been watching her too in those moments. She blushed then, but not from embarrassment. There was a heat in his gaze that made her imagine being pressed up against his bare chest, his lips trailing down her throat to the edge of her corset.

At lunch time, he chose to eat with the workers and get to know them and their duties. It was for the best, as far as Charlene was concerned. She couldn't bear the distraction of trying to share a meal with Jesse. He spent the rest of the day getting into the routine of the ranch, even working through dinner.

John insisted that Charlene take food to Jesse's quarters, despite her objections. When he said he was fatigued and would be retiring to bed; she conceded out of concern for his health rather than for Jesse's appetite. She wanted so badly to get out of her uncomfortable clothes and check on things with the employees—she knew they would divulge any worthy gossip about the new arrival. Instead, she did as she was told and walked to the outbuilding that served as guest quarters with a basket of food in her hands.

The door was partially open, and she could see him in the lamplight. His back was to her, and he stood in front of the wash basin shaving away a day's worth of stubble. He wore no shirt or boots, only a pair of clean denims. She watched as the defined muscles in his shoulders and back rippled with each movement he made with the straight razor.

After a moment he stopped, his eyes meeting hers in the mirror. Rinsing his face, Jesse turned, wiping the water away with a towel, damp strands of hair falling across his forehead.

Suddenly, her corset felt incredibly tight, and she was short of breath. *Dear Lord*, Charlene thought, *no man has any right to look that good.* Her eyes traveled the length of his chest to the waist of his trousers, which hung on his hips at a much too tempting level. His chest had the same golden tan as his face—he must have worked without a shirt quite often. She could picture him performing the strenuous tasks of the ranch, a gleam of perspiration enhancing each swell of muscle.

Heat crept into her face, and she started feeling lightheaded. "I...I brought you dinner," she breathed out. Why did the air seem so thin? It was getting harder and harder for her to drag it into her lungs. She took a few steps forward, setting the basket on the table.

Jesse shut the door and closed the distance between them. "Are you feeling all right?" he asked. "You look a little flushed."

"I'm fine...I just..." The room seemed to dim in front of Charlene's eyes. "Damn corset...I can't..." She wanted to say she couldn't breathe, but she wasn't sure the words had actually escaped her lips before everything went dark. She swore she could feel strong arms wrap around her, preventing her from hitting the floor.

Jesse carried Charlene to the guest bed and gently laid her down. He made quick work of unbuttoning the front of her dress and grabbed his boot knife from the side table, slicing the corset's lacing on both sides. He never understood why women tortured themselves with such a restricting garment and had seen too many suffer the consequences of the fashion. This woman had seemed uncomfortable from the moment they met, and he wondered if she normally adopted more practical clothing. The healthy sun glow of her skin told him she didn't spend her days doing needlepoint in the shade.

Now that the corset had been loosened, her breathing came easier. Jesse couldn't help but place his hand on her cheek as he watched her. He tried to tell himself it was to make sure some kind of fever wasn't causing her distress. Suddenly, he found himself brushing her bottom lip with his thumb. Her skin was like silk, and he wondered if her hair was just as soft. The space where her full lips parted was like an invitation to kiss her, but he held himself back as her eyelids fluttered, slowly opening to reveal her rich brown eyes.

"How are you feeling, Miss Solt?"

"Charley," she whispered. Was she delirious? Her eyes did still seem a bit glazed. Or was she mistaking him for someone else? That thought disturbed him.

"Everyone calls me Charley," she continued. "Except for Papa." Her gaze flickered around the room and back to him, and she seemed more aware of her situation. "What happened?"

"You fainted," Jesse told her, a slight smirk picking up the corner of his mouth. "Why you women insist on wearing corsets is a mystery to me."

Glancing down at herself, Charlene's gaze caught on the open front of her dress and the tattered laces of her corset. The realization of what had happened began to set in, and she sat up quickly, trying to cover herself. The movement placed her face mere inches from his. God, he smelled good. Like leather and soap.

"You should probably take it easy for a few more minutes," he said. The amusement vanished from his face and his voice sounded just a little deeper.

As he spoke, he moved even closer, and she could feel his warm breath on her lips. Charlene felt short of breath again and closed her eyes. This time she knew it wasn't the corset.

Jesse's mouth pressed against hers, gently at first. As her lips parted, he slid his tongue inside and heat instantly swept through her, settling low in her body. She ran her hands along his chest, so hard and masculine, sculpted from years of wrestling livestock to the ground. It made her think of him wrestling *her* to the ground, the two of them struggling for dominance as their skin touched, sparking even more passion between them.

She entwined her fingers in his hair and pulled him closer, deepening the kiss. Jesse slid his hands up her sides, loosening the corset even more as he progressed. He pulled the comb from her hair, allowing it to fall around her shoulders. He caressed her curls with his fingers as though testing their softness.

Jesse broke the kiss only long enough to move his lips down her throat, gently nipping along the way. Charlene issued a quiet gasp of pleasure. He unhooked the clasps holding together the front of the garment that had started this. Perhaps, she thought, it wasn't such a bad invention after all.

Freeing her breasts from the rigid boning, he trailed his kisses further down, wrapping an arm around her waist as she arched toward him. The fingers of his free hand found the hem of her skirts and stole underneath to follow the curve of her leg, brushing lightly against the inside of her thigh. Charlene desperately hoped he would slide further up to relieve some of the tension she felt building between her legs.

"You are so beautiful, Charley," he whispered between caresses.

Such a simple compliment, yet it shocked her back to reality. She froze.

Jesse pulled back to look at her. "What's wrong?"

"We can't do this," Charley gasped. "My father promised my hand to your employer."

"Without giving you a chance to know him?" The expression on his face was unreadable.

"I barely know *you*," she replied. "What's the difference? And I'm certain your boss will want his 'property' to remain intact."

Deep down she knew there was a big difference. She was extremely attracted to the man in front of her, whereas she might despise the man who was to arrive in a few short days. But she couldn't allow those thoughts to take seed in her mind. She had to think of her father's wishes for her well-being. "I'm sorry, I just can't."

Charley pushed past him, clasping the front of her dress together as she flung open the door and fled into the night toward the main house.

Jesse followed her path to the doorway, leaning against the jamb as he watched her go. He let out a heavy sigh and shifted the uncomfortable bulge pressing against the denim of his pants. It was going to be a long week.

For the next several days, Charlene abandoned her dresses once again for more practical attire. She needed the hard work to get her mind off of that first night. It wouldn't do any good to lust after a man she couldn't have. It was bad enough that, when the deal was finalized, Jesse would be a permanent fixture at the ranch.

As it was, Jesse seemed as unavoidable as her looming fate. He was around every corner as if he had been waiting for her, and on a few occasions, she accidentally brushed against him, stirring the flames once again.

Jesse even joined them for meals, at her father's request. John wanted to get to know more about the man who would be taking over the ranch, and Jesse was his only source of information.

The ranch hand tried to make it sound as though Forsythe was every bit the gentleman in all his ventures. But of course a loyal employee would say such things. Subtle cues in Jesse's expressions led Charlene to believe he was less than forthcoming. Things that made it look like he was ashamed of what he said. His inability to meet her gaze made her worry.

The evening before Forsythe was due to appear, she confronted Jesse in the doorway of the guest quarters as he was washing up from the day's work. Her timing was impeccable. He was shirtless again, and she had to strengthen her resolve.

"What is Mr. Forsythe *really* like?" she asked without preamble, irritation tightening her voice.

He turned to face her, and it was like the first night was repeating itself. Except now she wore a shirt, pants, and vest instead of the garments she would be expected to wear once again for the businessman's arrival in the morning.

"He's everything I've said him to be," Jesse replied, brows raised in curiosity as he walked toward her. "You'll see for yourself. He'll give you everything you need or want. He's been very fortunate with his investments."

Anger flooded Charlene in a hot torrent. "I don't care about his money! I don't want it," she exploded. "The only things that matter to me are already here. I love doing work on the ranch. Will he allow that? Or am I to be the dutiful wife and wear dresses and host parties? I want my father to be happy, but he's not unless I am. And I won't be happy! Not like that. And I want..."

She stopped, terrified of what she'd almost let slip. She turned and stalked through the doorway, heading toward the house. Halfway across the yard, something fell in front of her eyes before tightening around her arms and waist, nearly throwing her off balance. When she caught herself, she realized Jesse had lassoed her. Slowly, he pulled the rope, forcing her back to his doorway.

Once he had her all the way inside, he shut the door and grabbed her arms. He pressed her against the wall, his bare chest so close she could feel his heat.

"Tell me, Charley," he said huskily. "What else do you want?"

Her eyes widened, and her lips parted slightly as he ran a single finger down the side of her throat and over the swell of her breasts, finally cupping one in his palm while running his thumb over the material covering her nipple. The contact caused liquid heat to pool further south, and she could barely remember the question he had asked. He pressed into her further, his arousal brushing against her stomach.

"Tell me what you want, Charley," he whispered next to her ear, his breath feathering her jaw.

"I want you," she answered breathlessly. "Will he give me that?"

He pulled back slightly and looked at her with his captivating blue eyes.

"You have me right now." Without giving her a chance to respond, he brought his mouth down on hers, entering with his tongue.

This time, she didn't hold back, matching his passion with her own.

Jesse unbuttoned her vest, sliding it down her arms and letting it fall to the floor along with the lasso.

With her arms freed, Charley slid her hands from his muscled chest around his back, coming to rest on his tight backside. Pulling his hips closer, she could feel his erection grow harder against her.

Jesse groaned deep in his throat. He tugged at her shirt, yanking it free from her pants, breaking contact only long enough to pull it over her head. The garment fell carelessly to the floor as he lifted her hips to push his firm shaft against her core. Her nipples hardened as they brushed against his skin. The material remaining between them created a delicious friction, causing Charlene to grow even wetter.

As though Jesse could sense her arousal, he kissed a path to the fullness of her breasts, taking a nipple into his mouth and suckling it taut while stimulating the other with his fingers, nearly sending her over the edge.

Charley gasped and wrapped her legs around his waist, arched her back, and rubbed herself against his throbbing erection. Now the last bit of clothing they wore was becoming an annoyance, a barrier to be torn away.

Jesse cradled her in his arms and carried her to the bed, coming down on top of her. Moving his mouth to hers once again, he lifted first one of Charley's legs, then the other, to remove her boots. He slid down her body to unbutton her pants and pull them off in one smooth motion. Then he undid his own pants, allowing them to drop to the floor before stepping out of them and running his hands slowly up her legs. His steely cock skimmed against her sensitive flesh like the softest velvet, and just the sight of Jesse unleashed a fresh wave of moisture between Charley's thighs. She wanted to feel his thick arousal inside of her, filling her. But he didn't enter, and she thought the wait would be the death of her.

"Are you certain you want this? If we keep going, there's no turning back."

The look of concern in his eyes was enough to convince her. He must know as well as she what might happen should Forsythe realize she was no longer untouched. But she didn't care about the consequences.

"If I am to be miserable for the rest of my life, tied to someone I care nothing about, I want to have one night of happiness. I want my first time to be with you," she said quietly.

A hint of a smile touched his lips.

"You can be very persuasive. I promise to be gentle."

He reached to the side table and came back with a shiny boot spur in his hand. Before she could question him, Jesse began to lightly roll the spur along her breasts, tickling her erect tips with the rowel. He traced the curves of her ribs and stomach, leaving her caught between laughter and moaning. Moving further down, Jesse trailed along the tender flesh of her thighs, following the path with light kisses. Slowly, he spread her apart, running the chilled metal along her moistened slit.

Charlene bucked in exquisite torture as he rolled it up and down her clit with varying pressure. Before she found her release, Jesse dropped the spur on the floor and sank down, settling his mouth at her core. His tongue laved at her folds, and he sucked and nibbled at her aching mound, gently inserting one and then two fingers inside her. The combined sensations were unrelenting, and she cried out, her body trembling.

Before she could fully recover, Jesse moved up her body again and pressed the tip of his erection against her opening, slipping ever so slowly into her until he was sheathed nearly to his base.

Jesse stilled as Charlene became accustomed to the length of him. After the initial pressure had passed, she pushed herself even further down. She wanted everything he could give her. He pulled out nearly all the way before thrusting in again, and she could feel the tension escalating.

Jesse cupped her buttocks and lifted her, pressing their bodies together as he pushed harder into her, increasing the rhythm, leisurely at first, but growing in intensity. His pubic bone rubbed her mound as he moved, recreating what his mouth had done before. Charley's muscles clenched around him, and she was nearly frantic as she urged him on, not wanting to lose the sensation of him pumping in and out of her slick opening. Their combined shouts of release echoed as Jesse quickened his pace to an earth-shattering level, and she felt his cock jerk as he exploded inside of her. Together they collapsed in exhaustion, their bodies still spasming, reluctant to separate.

Over the next few hours, they enjoyed each other again and again, filling the night with tender heat. As the sky began to lighten, though, Charley knew she had to return to the house to prepare for Forsythe. As she dressed, tears burned her eyes.

Jesse brushed the hair from her neck and kissed her sensitized skin as she pulled on her boots.

"I wish he was you," she choked out as she slipped from his grasp.

She ran out before he could stop her.

In the morning, Charley stood on the porch with her father and Jesse as a wagon filled with trunks arrived. She couldn't meet Jesse's gaze, and she felt sick when she saw the only person on the wagon.

As promised, she had dressed much as she had that first day. She couldn't find her comb, though, so her hair hung loose.

Jesse wore what Charley figured was his Sunday best. He looked incredibly handsome. The man driving the wagon, however, was overweight and looked to be in his fifties. Just as she'd expected. Charley wanted to cry.

"You made good time, William," Jesse commented cheerfully.

"The trains were actually on schedule, if you can believe it." The other man chuckled. "I admit, I was rather shocked you came to a decision so quickly, Mr. Forsythe. I rather thought you would take another week or change your mind altogether. The telegram was a bit of a surprise."

Charley looked at Jesse in astonishment.

"What can I say, William? I know something good when I see it," he responded, looking directly at Charley when he spoke. "Mr. Solt? Charley? Allow me to introduce William Canton, my personal accountant."

"You're Forsythe?" Charley sputtered.

He strode toward her. "Your father knew you would react badly to my proposal. We've been communicating for months. He thought it best if you got to know the real me before I told you. Broadwell was my mother's maiden name. I use it when I don't want undue attention."

She stared at him in disbelief. He frowned slightly at her reaction. "Charley, please say something."

Tears began to flow down her face. His shoulders relaxed, and he raised his hands to bracket her cheeks while his thumbs smoothed away her tears. She placed her hands on his chest and felt something rigid in his pocket. It was her hair comb. He had been carrying it with him. "You're exactly what I want," she whispered.

She wrapped her arms around his neck and he swept her up, capturing her mouth with his and carrying her toward the guest quarters.

"Well," John said to William, "I guess the rest is just ceremony."

The two men laughed as they went inside the main house.

SMALL-TOWN FAMOUS

Lissa Matthews

W hat in the hell were you thinkin', Bethann?"

"I was thinkin' that little bitch better keep her hands off o' my man."

Tommy sighed and tried hard not to smile. He needed to stay stern with her. "You can't go 'round town totin' your shotgun like that. You shoulda known the sheriff would lock you up. For Chrissakes, Bethann, he's my boss!"

"He only caught me 'cause it was his precious little princess I was aimin' at." She snorted. "Well, that and someone called him. When I find out who, you better believe I'm gonna tan their hide. They'll be lucky if I don't fill it with buckshot."

Tommy shook his head at the woman behind the black iron bars. She sat on the bench on the far side of the cell with her arms crossed over her chest and her right leg crossed over her left. Bethann Pritchard was spitting mad.

He'd been in love with her all his life, and she with him, and never once in all their eighteen years together had she ever acted like this.

He slid his arms through the bars and linked his fingers. "Why are you so jealous all of a sudden?"

"Jealous? You think I'm jealous?" Bethann stood faster than lightning and stomped her way across the concrete floor to stand nose to nose with him. "Jealous ain't got nothin' to do with it, Tommy Martin."

"Then what does it have to do with? What's gotten into you?"

She tilted her chin in defiance, but it was just for show. He could see the angry tears in her eyes. "You like her, and I'm tired of her sniffin' around what ain't hers. Time for her to go back to wherever it is she came from."

If Tommy hadn't seen it for himself, he would never have believed it. Bethann was pouting. "I like ever'body, baby." Judging by her deepening scowl, that didn't even come close to appeasing her.

She kicked out at one of the bars, and he stepped back just in time. "But I see how you look at her."

Tommy pushed up his cowboy hat. He wanted to make sure he got a real good look at his woman during this conversation. He also wanted to make sure she could look him in the eyes without anything getting in the way. "And how do I look at her?"

Bethann dropped her gaze to the floor and dug the toe of her scuffed boot into a divot in the floor. "Like you want her," she mumbled.

He eyed her skeptically. "Uh-huh. Is that all?"

Her head whipped up so quick Tommy nearly had to take a step back. "Is that all? Ain't that enough?"

"Well, in all honesty here, I was expectin' a little more than that. That's not enough for you to go carryin' your daddy's double barrel down Main Street in the middle of the day, scarin' folks."

"Every single person in this town knows me, and I didn't scare anyone. Well, 'cept for her. I don't like the way you look at her ass in those little cut-off shorts and those tiny shirts. It's a wonder she wears anything at all. There'd be more left to the imagination if she was naked."

He contemplated her, his back teeth gnawing on the inside of his cheek, his mind doing everything it could think of to keep him from smiling. "So, is it that you're jealous 'cause I look at her ass, which *is* kinda hard to miss when she puts it in my face, or is it 'cause you wish you were still that young?"

"You son of a bitch."

"Your eyes are a bit greener than usual, baby doll." From the look on his lover's face, Tommy was damn glad to have the jail cell bars separating them. Where Bethann's temper was concerned, he knew a blessing when he saw it, and her not being able to get a hand on him when he made his confession was definitely a blessing.

Before he opened his mouth again, he backed away a couple steps. "I'm the one who called the sheriff."

"You what?" she asked, her voice dropping low and menacing.

He would pay for this when she was released and they got home—the narrowing of her eyes told him that—but he'd already known it the second he placed the call. "I called him and told him he needed to come get you."

"*You?* You had him put me in jail?"

Even though she was still speaking in that low tone that scared the bejesus out of everyone who knew her, he wouldn't show fear, and he wouldn't back down. "I did."

"Why?"

"It's his daughter you're jealous of and his daughter you bought the shotgun outta hock for. You're outta control."

She sneered. "You don't know the meanin' of out of control, but you just wait. When I get outta here, I'm gonna—"

God, she was full of piss and vinegar. There wasn't a woman on the planet who could hold a candle to her. He was so whipped. "No. This will be resolved while you're in there. I'm done walkin' on eggshells with you whenever another woman is in the same three feet of space I am. We're gonna settle this here and now."

"There's nothin' to settle."

"The hell there ain't."

She clucked her tongue and looked away. It was a few seconds before she spoke again. "I get it. You just don't want me anymore."

"What are you talkin' about?" The woman was out of her everloving mind.

She turned her head back toward him briefly, and that was when he spotted the fear and vulnerability in her pretty eyes. Bethann was never vulnerable, never scared of anything or anyone. She'd take on the devil himself without blinking an eye, but something had her spoiling for a fight. Something had her scared.

"You don't want me anymore, Tommy. I see it. You work all the time or go out with the boys. You look at the sheriff's daughter like she's dinner and you're a starvin' man, even though she's more'n ten years younger than you."

He was dumbfounded. "I don't know where in Sam Hill you got the idea I don't want you. I love you, Bethann. Always have. I don't get why you seem to doubt me now."

"Then why are you never around?"

The crazy gene, the one Southerners talk about having in their families, must have skipped a few generations and caught up with Bethann. He just couldn't wrap his head around why she was acting so damn foolheaded. "I ain't been gone any more this week than I've been gone any other week. Damn, woman. I play poker once a week. I bowl once a week. And I play ball on the weekends. I've always done that. You know I've always done that. So don't be givin' me shit about not bein' home." He took a deep breath. "As for the way I look at what's-her-name? If you were to see the way I look at you when you walk away from me, you wouldn't question anything. You're it for me."

She swallowed hard, then her eyes welled with tears. "Then why won't you marry me?"

He had to mentally take another step back and think before he spoke. "Marry? Who said anything about marrying you?"

"Exactly. You won't marry me. Why not?"

He tried to keep a straight face and not give her any hint of how lost he was in their conversation. "We've never even discussed marriage."

Bethann stomped her foot. "I know we haven't. I want to know why."

"Hell, woman, I don't know why. We live together, sleep together. We do all the things married people do. I guess I figured we were happy this way."

Her hands balled into fists at her sides. "Tommy Martin, you know damn good and well I've always wanted to have a life with you, with kids and the white picket fence. Well, I got the fence, but no kids and no wedding ring. Why don't you want to marry me?"

Tommy took his hat off and ran a hand through his hair. He wouldn't deny being confused as all hell. At least not to himself. As he'd told her, he'd just assumed that they'd live as they had ever since the day she graduated high school. Together. Forever.

He'd give her as many kids as she wanted. Give her damn

near anything at all, but she'd never told him she wanted to get married. Everyone in town knew they were a couple, knew they'd die a couple. Sure, some of the people talked about how he and Bethann lived in sin and were going to hell, but he'd never listened to them. Didn't think Bethann had either. Maybe he'd been wrong.

After all, they did live in a small town, and everyone's business was everyone else's.

"So, let me get this straight. You think I want someone else because I haven't married you yet? Even though the subject of marriage has never come up?"

"No. I said you don't want me anymore." She paused and bit her lip. "But do you? Want someone else?"

"Good God, really? All this because some girl keeps flashing her ass in Daisy Dukes?"

"I don't have her body," she grumbled, "and even I can admit she's hot."

"No, you don't have her body. You have yours, and I know every inch, every hill, every valley. And yeah, she is hot. So're a lot of other college girls, but that doesn't mean I want them. Shit, baby, you're all I want."

Her chin jutted higher. "Are you bored with me?"

She wasn't hearing a damn word he was saying. "Where'd that come from? Who said anything about bored?" He blew out an exasperated breath, but leaned closer to the bars. "You keep jumpin' from one thing to the other. I'm just not sure what you want here, Bethann. I love you. Since I was ten years old, I've loved you. I knew that day you walked into the school, holdin' your mama's hand, lookin' so sweet and so scared, that I was gonna spend my life with you. I've never seen you look scared, not since that day, not until now."

Her mouth trembled. "I don't want to lose you, Tommy.

Not to some wannabe cowgirl."

"You're not gonna lose me," he said softly. "And so far as what you said about me lookin' at her, yeah, I look. Doesn't mean I want inside her shorts. Shit, I've never gone after any of the cowboys and ranch hands you've stared after."

The guilty flush that lit her cheeks was all the answer he needed. For the first time in their long relationship, someone new had showed up in town and took an interest in what Bethann considered her personal property. Not that women hadn't shown an interest in him before. But they'd all known he belonged to Bethann and that nothing and no one was gonna take him away from her. The sheriff's little girl...she didn't know all that, and even if she did she wouldn't have cared.

She was interested in him, and Bethann had taken it poorly. Now she was talking nonsense and wanting marriage and reassurance.

He knew Bethann looking at the cowboys had no bearing on their relationship. He knew she was his and would never do more than admire from afar. Deep down inside, she knew he wouldn't stray either. But for some reason, her feathers were ruffled.

He kind of liked her this way, though. All hot and bothered and jealous. Not for the fact she seemed genuinely upset, but for the fact that she was willing to do anything to protect what they had together.

It didn't hurt that her hair was a wild mess, that her shirt was wrinkled with a few buttons undone down the front, or that her shorts showed off her strong, tanned legs. A few hours in the slammer just made her hotter than hell to him.

He eyed her from head to toe, taking in every beautiful inch. "You know everyone's gonna be talkin' about you bein' in jail."

She snorted and tossed back her hair. "They wouldn't have anything to talk about if you hadn't called the sheriff."

"You're right. But dammit, Bethann, you've been goin' off half-cocked since that little girl came into town, and it has to stop. You scared the poor thing half to death."

"Then she shoulda kept her hands to herself. I already told you that."

He knew he really ought to end the conversation now that it was going in circles, but she looked so damn cute with her face turning red and her eyes sparkling with anger. "It's not like I was encouragin' her," he murmured, knowing he was just feeding the fire.

"You weren't *dis*couragin' her either," she said, her voice getting snippy.

"So this is what it's really about then? You bein' jealous? You ready to admit it?"

"If you'd had a ring on your finger, she wouldn't have been messin' around you."

Tommy ducked his head and hid his smile. He fished the jail cell keys from his back pocket and jangled them in front of her before sliding a key into the lock.

Her eyes widened. "You had those all this time? And you're just now lettin' me out? When I get my hands on you..."

"You're not gonna do anythin'," he said, soft and dark as he stepped into the eight-by-ten cell. He advanced on her until she'd backed herself into the bars on the adjacent wall. "You're gonna listen and you're gonna listen real good, baby." He took her hands, one by one, and lifted them to the bars above her head. "Don't let go until I tell you that you can. Got it?"

She nodded, her eyes still wide, questioning. He knew his demeanor had changed in a split second, but he'd bet every dime they had in the bank she was soaking wet between her thighs because of it.

He let go of her arms and got to work on the buttons of her shirt. What was left of them, anyway. One by one, he slipped them through the little loops until her shirt was wide open. Her full, heavy breasts filled the lacy bra nicely, and as much as he wanted at her bare skin, he'd make do with tracing the edge of the material with his fingertips.

Bethann shivered and moaned as he got closer to her nipples and although he wanted to touch them, tease them, he didn't. "I don't want another woman," he started softly, staring into her eyes while his fingertips began moving down her sides and across her stomach. "Not the sheriff's daughter. Not Maxine in the diner. Not Dixie at the car dealership. Not your mama over at the bank." He popped the snap on her shorts and felt the quiver in her belly. "I want you, Bethann. Only you." The zipper was next, giving way at the insistence of his fingers. "You wanna get married? Fine. I'll marry you before the courthouse closes today. You wanna get started on kids? We'll do that right now. You wanna stamp a brand on me? All you gotta do is say so, and I'll let you put it wherever you want."

He slid his hand down the front of her shorts and found her just the way he knew he would: soaked and scalding hot. They both groaned when his finger grazed her clit just before sliding up inside her. "Some new girl in town isn't gonna turn my heart away from you. I don't care how smokin' hot she is. You're mine and I'm yours."

The last was said against her lips just before he crushed them with his own. Her body strained against him, her hips thrusting up into his hand, and his tongue speared into her mouth much like his finger was doing inside her pussy.

He wrapped his tongue around hers and urged it into his mouth for a good hard sucking, for a chance to nip at it with his teeth. She lit him up inside, always had. The way she responded to him was as unique as the way he responded to her. He wanted her as much today as he had the first time she surrendered her kisses to him. He'd waited for her to be ready, to be of age. He'd waited, but she'd thrown herself at him more times than he could count, and the fiery temper she'd always displayed when he'd pushed her away was just as scorching as the passion was when he'd finally relented.

She'd thrown herself against him so hard it had taken his breath away, that day and every day since. She gave him every-thing. He would never betray her.

Right now she was giving him everything he wanted. She was up on the toes of her boots one second, pushing her cunt into his touch, but then she was back on her heels trying to fight the orgasm he knew would claim her before too long.

Tommy nibbled her tongue hard enough to make her squeal, then let go. He drew deep, silent breaths as he watched her gasping when their lips parted. With his free hand he pushed at her shorts and she wiggled enough to get them down to her ankles, then over her boots. She kicked them away.

"So, what's it gonna be, darlin'? Marriage before five?"

"You..." She gasped, her eyes blinking hard. "Are you serious?"

He popped the buttons on his Levi's and pulled his cock out. He was hard as steel, his blood pounding through the engorged shaft, his balls heavy. He needed desperately to be inside her.

He hitched one of her legs around his waist, and with his honey-coated fingers, positioned his cock at her entrance. His gaze connected with hers as he slowly pushed upward, filling her, screwing himself into her with a swivel of his hips. "I would never joke or tease you about marriage." With one hard surge, he pushed himself into the heated walls that had always fit him like a glove. "I am yours and only yours, Bethann."

He pressed her into the bars long enough for her to get her other leg up so she could lock her boots together. Then, gripping the bars on either side of her hands, he gave her short, pointed thrusts that kept her in position. He pounded her, dipped his hips and ground into her, watching her pupils dilate as her hunger rose.

Being with her like this never got old, never failed to suck him in. His love for her knew no limits—and neither did his lust. It was love at first sight for him and the feeling had never waned.

She drew in a quick breath, and her voice snagged on her need to cry out. He knew her, knew she was fighting the wild streak that ran deep. "Let it go, baby. No one else is here. No one'll hear," he murmured against her lower lip as he nibbled on it.

"Th-they will. They...they always know when we..."

She was right about that. The people in their small town always knew when they were getting dirty in places they shouldn't be. The memories only made him harder, thrust faster, grunt louder.

The church balcony during choir practice.

The old treehouse down by the lake before the town picnic.

The Fourth of July float just a few months ago. God, they'd been caught butt-assed naked going at it on a tractor seat. Didn't matter that it was his tractor that was being used...

"I love it when people know, darlin'." He nipped at her jaw and up to her ear. "You love it when people know, too," he whispered right before he bit down on the lobe.

She bucked against him and screamed his name. It echoed off the concrete block walls, and her pussy began contracting on his dick. The muscles in her arms tightened, and her hands held so tight to the bars above her head that her knuckles turned white.

He loved watching her come apart. She gave everything in the way she flexed her thighs against his hips, in the way she gripped his cock with her body, her muscles milking him, coaxing him to join her in letting go and flying free. Her booted heels dug into his ass, and he lurched forward, attaching his mouth to hers. He wanted to swallow her bliss and pleasure. The kiss ravished her as much as his steely cock did, a reaffirmation of his need for her.

"Let go of the bars," he whispered against her mouth, unwilling to let go of any part of her, but wanting to feel her completely wrapped around his body.

She dropped her arms and slid them across his shoulders. She trailed her mouth over his cheek and buried her face in his neck. "Yes," she said between little bites and sucks of his skin.

"Yes?" He was momentarily lost.

"Marry me."

His cock strained inside her cunt as happiness surged through him. He fucked her, taking her body with every ounce of strength he had. She held him tight within her arms and legs, curving herself to fit him.

"You askin' me?" He didn't really care if she was asking or telling. He was closing in on his orgasm and finding it hard to think. Pretty soon, he wouldn't be able to do more than grunt and shake as he unloaded inside her wet heat.

"I am." She lifted her head and brought her hands up to hold his face between her palms. "Will you marry me, Tommy?"

And that was it for him. He'd had no idea the thought of marrying the woman he'd spent his life with, loving with his whole heart, would have such impact on him, but hell if it didn't. He nodded as come flowed from his balls through the shaft of his cock to fill her. "Yes," he hissed, the painful bliss of such a hard orgasm taking his breath away and forcing his eyes closed.

He'd had no idea this was what he'd wanted until she asked. He shuffled forward a smidge and pressed her hard into the bars, enough that there'd be impressions from them in her back. He didn't care. He'd soothe them.

She kissed the tip of his nose in a tender gesture, and he smiled. "I love you, Tommy," she said softly against his ear.

"Thank God for that, baby," he panted, trying to gather his breath. She giggled, and he smiled into her hair. "I love you, too. No more jealousy?"

Bethann sighed dramatically. "Oh I don't know. The make-up sex was kinda good. I kinda like doin' it in jail."

Tommy laughed and began untangling her from around him. He let her slide down the front of his body. "That it was. We can cross it off our list."

"Think people will talk?" she asked with a grin as she righted her clothes.

"Yeah, people will talk. We'll definitely make the morning edition." He tucked his slicked-up dick back into his jeans and buttoned them. "Bethann?"

She looked up, soft and sated and a beautiful wreck from their little tussle. "Yeah?"

"You mean it? 'Bout gettin' married?"

"Yep. Soon as you get me outta here, we're beatin' the pavement to the courthouse."

He stepped aside and made a grand sweep of his arm toward the open cell door. "Then by all means, lead the way."

Bethann wrinkled her nose and stuck her tongue out at him. "I always do."

Tommy laughed and bent to pick up the hat she'd thrown

to the floor. Yeah, she always did, and it was what made her famous in their small town. She blazed her own trail, did her own thing, had since she was seventeen. He'd been by her side from the beginning and would be until the end.

Slapping the hat on his head, he took long strides to catch up with her. He didn't want to be late for his own wedding.

THE STORM

Tahira Iqbal

The storm arrives with wild abandon, twisting and turning, gray fury unleashing torrential rain that blurs the horizon.

"I don't think you should drive in this weather, Candace!" my friend says from the covered deck.

I shrug away her concern, tossing my jacket over my head, and run for my car.

"I'll be fine, Renee!" I yell over the rumbling. "Thanks for lunch!"

Soaked to my ankles, I start the SUV I borrowed from my daddy—my car is at the dealership after a suspicious rattle under the hood demanded attention. I switch on the wipers, which beat rapidly across the windshield but barely make a dent in the deluge.

I wave to Renee, hoping that she can see me, and maneuver up the drive to the main road.

Borrowing the SUV was a good idea, but taking the back roads isn't. Water gathers against the body of the powerful vehicle as I drive through a flooded dip in the road, the engine growling menacingly as it chokes on the rainwater.

"Come on, baby..." I nudge the gas, my heart pounding against my ribs as the beast climbs, clearing the water. Miles of fork lightning ignite the sky, showing me eerie black clouds.

I'm about eight miles from my apartment in town when the phone rings. I activate the hands-free system. The connection's patchy, but my daddy's distinct voice peppers over the line.

"I'm okay," I say, speaking over him, hoping he can hear me, "I'm on my way home."

"...road is under two foot of water... Don't go to..."

"Road? Which road? I can't hear you!"

"Stay at Renee's..." he says. "...not safe...under..." More crackles. "...two foot of water..."

The line disconnects suddenly as a giant whip of lightning snaps across the sky. I try to play connect the dots with my daddy's words and come to the realization that I should indeed turn back to Renee's. In the act of searching for a place to turn the SUV around, I'm distracted by rushing movement in front of the windshield.

"What the...?"

Panicked horses bolt toward me. I can see a broken fence behind them. My gut reaction is to wrench the wheel hard left to avoid them, and I hit the brake with both feet at the same time. The SUV skids on the surface water, sending me toward the edge of the road, and I careen down a hillside.

"Oh God..." The air bag explodes open as I slam to a stop at the bottom. My head cracks backward, smashing off something hard. The impact is enough to show me stars, and more worryingly, I see water rising over the hood.

Lazy hands try to work the seat belt, but there's an urgent need to close my eyes. With a breathy sigh of horror, I'm drawn

into an unconsciousness I'm helpless to fight. The last thing I see
is blood dripping into my eye.

Arms—strong, sure and wet—reach around my frame, pulling
me up and out of the haunting stillness.

"It's okay. I've got you." Rain beats down on the roof of the
car like a drum; the smell of overheated metal is in the air. It's
acrid and catches the back of my throat.

"What happened?" I cough.

"You were in an accident." The voice is male, deep, authoritative, and utterly familiar.

"Brent...?" I whisper. "Is that you?"

"Hold onto me, darlin'." He adjusts my weight, bringing me
up against his chest once we clear the cab.

My arms obey, going around his neck, vision filling with
lightning, blinding me for a moment until my sight is then
consumed by eyes that shine with equal power.

"I've got you," he says again.

Brent easily carries my weight up the bank, using a guide
rope tossed down by someone on the road. We go slowly and
steadily, his strength almost mythological against the storm.
Horse hooves clip rapidly on the pavement, sharp bellows of
fear rising from the scattered herd.

I'm on my feet, Brent's hands on my elbows for stability.

"Easy..."

I look up to take in the violent heavens lighting up all around
us, the rain stinging the wound on my head.

"You're okay." His hand smooths back the strings of hair
sticking to my face.

I look down the ravine at the car, the hood crushed, water
flowing into the cab.

"You're all right now."

I'm awed by the moment, the storm, the crash, seeing my ex again after so long and under this awful dark sky.

I mean to say something, but my knees unlock; Brent's arms envelop me before I hit the road.

When I wake, I'm in a bed, nude and with a headache that shakes my back teeth. My fingers reach for the small bandage tugging my hair line; my eyes adjust to the delicate light in the room. I sit up slowly, pushing away the nausea in my stomach with long, deep breaths. I hug the sheets, cosseted also by the roaring fire set in the hearth at the side of the room.

Oh God. I've been in this bed before, but never alone.

Affected by the location, I leave the linens behind, heading to the bathroom, willing my legs to obey and keep me upright.

I grimace as I see the blush of a bruise at my temple, and there's an equally terrific gathering of color starting at my collarbone and ending at my right hip. The seatbelt saved my life...and so did Brent.

The door in the room opens. I search for a towel, dragging the folded bath sheet around my frame and edge out.

Six-feet-six of recognizable perfection with eyes as gray as the storm stare at me as if I'm an apparition.

Brent's wearing faded blue denims and the leather belt I bought him for our first Christmas together. His shirt is pure white cotton; I know what that feels like under my fingertips, soft with age, scented like the earth from hard work, but mostly of the designer cologne I also gave him that year.

"You should be resting."

I can't respond, captivated as I am by the man who always moved with such authority.

"I would've put you in one of the barns, but there was a last minute rush of bookings. Tourists couldn't get out of town because of the storm."

I nod my understanding; Brent's mom had converted the derelict barns on her property into five-star guest houses that were booked out most of the year.

"Um. Who undressed me?" I ask as the quiet lingers.

His gaze is unyielding. His damp hair catches the light. "It's not like I haven't seen you naked before."

"Brent..." I start.

"What the hell were you thinking?" His voice is suddenly hard, coarse with stress. "You shouldn't have been driving in a storm like this!"

The strength of his concern reminds me of a moment we'd shared today; I'd roused, worried by my predicament, in the cab of his vehicle as he drove back to the ranch. I'd sighed, held onto his corded biceps, moved by the fact that the only man I'd ever loved had saved my life.

Something blooms inside of my chest, making me choke back tears.

With a soft, realizing breath, he says, "Come down, okay? Mom's cooking up a storm. No pun intended."

I laugh softly, glad the tension has broken. "I'll need something to wear...?"

A smile dawns over his lips as his gaze roves my bare shoulders. "Here—your clothes are still in the wash." He reaches into the wardrobe, lifts out one of his shirts, and leaves me to it.

As I stand by the dresser to change, I notice a framed photograph of Brent and me cuddled close, watching the Fourth of July fireworks overhead. I trace a fingertip against the glass. My copy lives in a closet in my spare room.

Stiff and sore, I make my way downstairs, greeted by the scent of bread fresh from the oven and by Mrs. Williams, who fusses as if I haven't been out of her life for nearly six months.

"Thank God you're all right! Now, your daddy knows you're here, so don't worry about that, okay?" A huge rumble of thunder rattles the window panes. "I've assured him you're going to be just fine and told him to stay put. The man was half out of his mind with worry."

"It's still that bad out there?" She touches my brow with gentle fingers, but it just makes me teary-eyed. She's always been so nice to me.

"Sit, sweetheart, eat something."

There's a rapid knock at the back door; Mrs. Williams gets distracted by a ranch hand who's been brave enough to cross the yard to the main house.

"Help yourself to anything you need." She reaches for her waterproof jacket. "I'll be back soon."

I fix myself a plate of home-baked bread and make a large cup of hot, sweet tea. I close my eyes, not enjoying the headache, but savoring the taste of the bread and the knowledge that I've had a lucky escape.

When I open them, Brent is there, watching me from the door.

"How are you feeling?"

I nod carefully, holding up my bread. "Better. This is helping."

He cuts a piece for himself, takes the knife, and slathers a generous daub of peanut butter on it.

"I hope you don't mind, but I borrowed socks and"—I blush—"a pair of your boxers."

He leans against the counter rather than taking a seat. "They always did look better on you." Brent's words send heat through my pelvis, though really they shouldn't.

An awkward silence stretches between us and is finally broken by an almighty curl of lightning, followed by a huge peel of thunder that resonates in my belly.

Suddenly, Mrs. Williams is tapping hard on the glass window facing the yard, getting Brent's attention. He reaches for his jacket and heads out without a word.

I go upstairs, my heart aching. I stop and stare at the bed I woke up in, nervous like it might bite me, but when exhaustion tugs at my senses, I lay down, sobbing.

Movement in the room wakes me an hour later. "Brent?" I squint against the lamp light.

"It's okay. Go back to sleep."

"What happened? You're soaking wet!"

He quickly unbuttons the shirt and drags it off his shoulders, revealing a body precisely carved by his physical work outdoors. "Lightning struck one of the barns."

"Is everyone okay?"

He reaches for something in the wardrobe, and then starts to unbuckle his belt, sending my heart into my throat as he disappears into the bathroom.

"It didn't start a fire," he says through the wall. "We're okay."

He reappears wearing only sweats, his chest magnificently bare. Something deep inside me undulates, reminding me that I've had my hands on that skin, that I've had his delicious weight on top of me for hours.

"You risked your life," I whisper.

He shrugs his shoulders as if to say "no big deal."

"Brent...you saved my life." I kick out of the comforter, putting myself right in front of him, palming his wet hair, tracing the drops rolling down the curve of his shaded jaw.

He groans, stilling my hand under his. "Don't do this unless you mean it. When we broke up, Ace..."

The shirt I'm wearing only reaches to mid-thigh, so I guide his hand under it until he gets the hint and cups my ass, the hard press of his erection against my belly. "I love it when you say my name like that."

Brent weaves his hand into my hair, bringing his mouth to mine, the kiss burning my senses as his tongue enters my eager, open mouth.

All too soon he pulls away. "Bed. Now."

I stumble back to the covers as Brent kicks the door shut and locks it.

He finds home between my shaking legs, his lips on mine, his hand disappearing into the boxers, but this time at the front, where he rubs slowly, ever so slowly, in the gathering wetness.

My gasp of delight doesn't change his speed or pressure. My orgasm is a slow ride that snakes to the top of its peak before exploding outward.

I sink back, bumping the headboard.

"Careful, darlin'. I want you awake for the rest of the night." A lovely smile spreads across his features, illuminated by the small lamp that's showing me only inches of his skin.

I nuzzle his hard shoulder. The eroticism of the moment has brought my nipples to a tight peak.

He pushes the shirt up and over my head before focusing his attention on one nipple, enveloping it with his mouth. "Beautiful, as always."

I wind my hands into his hair as he starts to trace his lips down my body until he reaches my belly button, his fingers catching the boxers and pushing them down.

He kisses the sensitive skin of my inner thigh, leaving me trembling with the expectation of his journey as he strips me completely.

Soft kisses scorch my most intimate parts as Brent rises to draw his sweats off, finally showing me his incredible arousal.

"When I saw you in the SUV... I thought..." His eyes glitter suddenly as his fingers trace the bruise on my skin from the seatbelt. He positions himself on top of me.

I caress the side of his face in slow, teasing slides, widening my legs to create the space we need. "You've got me now... I'm here."

Brent reaches down, holding himself so that he can slide into me. Once inside, he waits a moment, as do I, enjoying the perfect fit we've always had.

I palm his taut backside as he begins thrusting, deep and sure, knowing that I've always loved his rhythm, that it always drives me insane with pleasure.

There's never any talk, no need for carnal encouragement. It's with silence that Brent and I make love.

"Keep your eyes open," he says. "I want to see what I've missed so much."

He comes deep inside me as I vault into another sensational climax that forces the breath out of my lungs.

Later, as I rest against Brent's chest, I'm able to hear his relaxed heartbeat against my ear. He's lit a few candles around the room now that the storm has knocked out the power.

"The last time I saw you was at Duke's wedding." Brent's fingers trail through my hair.

"I know." I think about the tremor that had raced through my heart as Brent's brother had married Renee; I was her maid of honor, Brent the best man, and we'd broken up only a month before.

"I kept my distance."

"We both did. We didn't want to ruin their day."

He reaches for my wrist, rubbing the inside flesh softly. "It damn near killed me when we had to dance together." He kisses my bruised forehead, the touch bringing pleasure rather than pain.

"It was a bitch," I say with an exaggerated sigh. "You kept standing on my toes."

I feel Brent's deep laugh through my whole body as a wonderful vibration.

"You know, I would imagine you here with me," he says quietly.

I shift onto my side, facing Brent.

"I would imagine touching you, the way you like it..." His hand disappears under the sheets, palming me gently between the legs.

With his gaze welded to mine, our silence grows. His ability to be silent yet utterly powerful is something I've always found fascinating about him. I'd watched Brent from the comfort of the house as he broke in horses...his patience, his utter dedication and endless determination, now focused on me.

"Why the hell did we break up, Ace?" He leans in to kiss me gently.

"I was scared," I whisper softly.

"Of what, darlin'?"

"Of this. Feeling so..." Tears sting my eyes

Brent smiles, "In love?"

I exhale, feeling a strange weight lifting off my shoulders. "You get it?"

"I get you. Always have, always will. I was just waiting for you to come back to me—although I could have done without you scaring me half to death in the process."

"Brent..." I welcome his lips back to mine, enjoying the strokes from his hand between my legs. When I come, the waves of my orgasm beat furiously against my nerves.

Giving me no time to get my breath back, he gently draws my legs apart and enters me. We make love until the wet, quiet dark of morning.

I wake just before dawn, Brent behind me, his arm over my hip, offering me shelter in such a comforting way. Gently, I draw his arm off to slide away from him.

I shower, then return to the room. Brent's awake, propped up against the headboard.

"Good morning." He drags the sheets aside, flashing me that beautiful body and kissing me boldly as he heads for the bathroom.

I hear the shower switch off no more than a minute later. Thinking nothing of it, I reach for my borrowed shirt, but instead stop in my tracks as I feel his hands on my hips.

"You don't need this." He reaches for the knot in the towel and unhooks it throwing it to the bed, "Here..." He takes my hands, placing them on the dresser, the photograph no longer making my heart smart.

The sensation of his big body pushing up and into mine makes me loop my hand around his neck to keep us as close as possible. I don't care that the bruise across my chest is protesting as his thrusts gain momentum.

Brent cups my breasts, rubbing the nipples between his fingers as warmth spills from him, leaving me fighting an orgasm so strong that I have to close my eyes.

An hour later, from the comfort of the bed, I hear encouraging shouts from outside. I loop sheets around me, following the sounds to the window.

Brent is standing at the open doors of the barn, horses racing past him into the wide, sun-drenched field, the sky utterly blue and clear of clouds. He cracks a rope, ensuring the animals get the spark they need to run and stretch their legs.

I see Mrs. Williams, clipboard in hand, talking to a ranch hand on a ladder assessing the sizable cracks in the roof's shingles. In the distance, there's a repair crew mending the fence that had allowed the horses to escape and run into my path.

Some inner sense makes Brent turn to the window and touch a finger to the brim of his hat, his smile as bright as mine. He hands the rope to another cowboy, jumps the fence, and lopes toward the house.

Moments later, he's in front of me, tugging the sheets away and pushing me back toward the bed.

He reaches for his belt, the coolness of the metal scraping my skin. "Ace," he says softly. "Ace."

And something inside me fixes right into place.

CAUGHT UNAWARES

Nena Clements

Get away!"

Squeals and screams pierced the peaceful afternoon air. Reece glanced up from stringing wire in time to see a figure dart down the hill. Arms flaying and hands brushing about the head, it made a beeline for the pond. A plunge and the expected splash of water ramped up his curiosity.

Dropping his tools, Reece ran the thirty feet to the pond's edge, shucking off his gloves along the way. The interrupted quiet of the water's surface shimmered in the afternoon sun. From beneath its surface emerged one surprising female.

"Lacy Wills, what the hell do you think you're doing?"

She wore a pair of old breeches and some old shirt. Almost looked like a boy coming off that hill, except for all those curves.

Sheets of water rolled off her chestnut curls and clothes as she emerged from the pond. Water plastered the thin cotton shirt against every swell and valley of her body. The boy's pants, too wide for her narrow waist, hung low over well-rounded hips and firm buttocks.

Reece couldn't breathe. Every daydream he'd conjured about Lacy the past year stared him in the face. He felt an involuntary surge of blood to his groin. She was more beautiful than he'd ever imagined.

Her head tilted back to allow the water to run from her face as she smoothed the excess moisture from her hair. His brain still hadn't fully engaged after the rush of lust taking hold of his body when her eyes opened and pinned him to the spot.

"What are you looking at, Reece?"

Damn. Heat flooded his cheeks. He shouldn't be ogling his best friend's sister. Hell, his body shouldn't be reacting like this either. He fought the urge to glance down and see how obvious his attraction to her was.

"Just wondering why you'd come running down the hill screaming like a banshee. And why are you dressed like that?"

A toss of her head moved body parts he shouldn't have been eyeing.

"I was after honey from that beehive in the big oak. I can't very well climb in a bustle. I'd just dipped a finger in when they swarmed on me." She swatted at the air around her head. "Can't you see them?"

Come to think of it, there were a few bees buzzing close by.

"So a dip in the pond should scare them away. I get it. C'mon out, Lacy. You're safe now." Reece stepped closer to the edge and extended his arm.

"I can climb out on my own."

Hitching her breeches to her waist, she began slogging toward the shore—and sank in over her head. Could've been a hole, but Reece wasn't taking any chances. Muscles tensed, he dove, boots and all, into the water.

Reece surfaced with Lacy, his hands circling her small waist. Her body was way too close. Her round doe eyes peered back at him as he found his footing on the slippery pond bottom.

Lacy sputtered and wriggled as she surfaced. Reece realized that the placement of his hand was less than appropriate—it had somehow slipped over the outer edge of her left breast. If the sight of her hadn't sent him over the edge, that simple touch did. His cock became ram-rod hard.

Thing was, he couldn't move his hand right away. She was suspended in the water, feet dangling by his knees, and shifting her would press all those luscious curves against his chest and groin. Lord knew, he didn't need her bumping up against that. Damn. Not now.

Her body softened in his hands. Doe eyes met his gaze, and her small hands grappled for his arms as a weighted hush stretched between them. He saw a rosy flush cover her sun-kissed cheeks, but it could've been the dunking.

Reece needed to break the tension. "Are you all right?"

"I will be when you put me down." A deeper shade of red infused her cheeks.

"Promise you won't drown?" He lowered her feet to the bottom and slid his hand past the sensuous curve of her breast. Watching for any reaction, he grimaced when Lacy thinned those full lips of hers and cocked a brow.

Setting her deeper in the water didn't improve his predicament. The loose tails of her shirt floated up and the buttons at the top opened to reveal the thin fabric of her chemise as it caressed her tantalizing cleavage. His eye roved over every inch of her. Her lush form set a fire inside him.

Once she regained her footing, Reece released his hold on her waist.

But Lacy's fingers circled his wrist and gave his arm a fierce tug. The force of it pulled him off his feet. Before his head slipped into the water, a smirk lit up her eyes.

"What the hell," he sputtered as his head broke the surface. "I'm only trying to help, Lace. You don't have to drown me in the process."

"I didn't ask you for any help." Hands on her hips, she breathed a gust of air. Those brown eyes threw fire at him.

Reece struggled to get his feet under him, the water in his boots giving him fits. He still hadn't righted himself when Lacy pushed through the water toward him. What was she doing?

She wore that same half smile she always seemed to get when she'd conjured some mischievous, daring joke to play on her brother Thad. That never boded well.

Reece raised one brow at her approach, wary of her volatile nature. A feather could have knocked him over when Lacy grabbed the front of his shirt and leaned into him. Her chocolate eyes held his gaze, then shifted to his mouth. His mouth turned dry as she leaned in close and swept her pink tongue the length of her full bottom lip before brushing a tentative kiss across his mouth.

A low moan escaped his throat as she pulled away. She tasted of honey and smelled of damp wildflowers. A timid tilt of her mouth and a sparkle in her eye betrayed her own pleasure in the act.

Instinctively, Reece circled his arms around her shoulders and drew her closer. Lacy yielded, molding her body into his and tilting her face up. Dipping his head, he angled his mouth over her warm lips and pressed a heated kiss on her mouth. The contact of their bodies and the intimacy of their mouths scorched the damp surface of his skin. He could have sworn steam rose from the water droplets.

Reece was aware of nothing but Lacy and the way her hands

trailed up the muscles of his back and her fingers as they dug into his shoulders. Her body pressed into his, and all he felt was the delicious pressure of her curves against his hard chest and the softness of her skin as his hands dug beneath her shirt.

She kissed him with equal fervor, hard and demanding. Emboldened by her confidence, Reece nudged his tongue against her lip, enticing her to open to him. Her soft lips parted, and his tongue slid against hers, warm and wet. Lacy moaned an answering sigh as his tongue swept deeper into her mouth, tangling with hers. Her grasp on his shoulders tightened as she met his every thrust with equal vigor. Tension built inside him as the taste of honey mingled with Lacy.

Beneath the water's surface, one slender leg twined around his as she used the soaked denim of his pants to climb up his body. Reece cupped his hand under the curve of her bottom and hoisted her up. Willowy legs draped in dripping wet canvas twined around his waist, clinging to him as if for dear life.

Lord, he had died and gone to heaven to have Lacy Wills wrapped around him like a snake in an oak tree.

Lacy clung to Reece for dear life. When her brain cleared from the haze of lust engulfing her, she realized she had wrapped herself around the man as if he were a mighty oak. It was all she could do when she saw him sluice through the water. Every corded muscled rippled beneath the wet shirt clinging to his skin. Shining drops of water twinkled on his tanned arms, and the tufts of hair that protruded from the neck of his wet shirt sent shivers of need quivering deep inside her.

All those years she'd known Reece McCord, worshiped him even, came crashing in on her. She was just the younger sister of his best friend. She had always thought he looked like the vision of those Greek gods she'd read about in school.

Today he was a Greek god incarnate. His sandy hair lay pasted against a high forehead. Golden green eyes shone as he brushed pond water from his face. Her first reaction was to taunt him as she usually did. But something inside clicked, and all the hints and suggestions the man had either ignored or just plain not seen made her ache once more for his acceptance. This opportunity could not be sacrificed. Lacy seized it, with both hands and most of her body.

When her mouth brushed against Reece's, she was sure she could have knocked him over with a feather. He seemed to go limp next to her. She was afraid she had underestimated the attraction—until Reece grabbed her with such desperation she thought he might never let her go. Not that she ever wanted him to. Two long years of flirtatious bumps, batted eyes, and punches in the arm, any sane man would have seen clearly how much she liked him...at least a little.

Nothing she had done elicited any sort of response. She was Thad's baby sister, and she guessed Reece saw her only as that.

But not today.

Today, she wanted to show him she was a woman. She *had* to pick the one day she'd dressed in Thad's breeches and shapeless shirt for a tomboy adventure—hunting wild honey. The wild mass of chestnut waves around her head was tied back with a leather thong for convenience. She hadn't even dragged a brush through it before leaving the house.

And now Reece kissed her with such fervor and hunger, she could faint for the sheer joy of it all. Her tongue tangled with his, and his large hands hoisted her up over his slim hips. With her ankles locked around his back, she hung on for dear, sweet life.

"Oh, Reece," she breathed as they broke for short gasps of air.

"Lacy," he growled, his forehead pressed to hers and his yellow eyes staring at her. "Thad is going to kill me."

"Thad has no part in this, Reece." She threaded her hands in his hair and pulled his head closer to her.

"Oh, yes." Reece broke again. "He told me never to touch you." His hands spread the width of her back, their heat evaporating the moisture of her shirt at their placement.

"You didn't touch me. I touched you." She feathered kisses over the golden skin of his cheeks.

Tiny lines crinkled at the edges of his eyes as he pulled back and smiled at her. "Not like I haven't thought about it for years, Lacy."

"Could've fooled me."

Her hands bracketed his handsome face as she peppered his mouth with tender kisses. They trailed over his nose and cheeks, his stubbled chin, and down the thick column of his throat.

"Carry me out, Reece," she breathed against the pulse at his throat.

Reece moved his hands to rest beneath her behind as she circled her arms around his neck and pressed herself closer to him. He strode effortlessly to the grassy shore. The hard planes of his chest crushed against her breasts, making the rough weave of her shirt rasp against the tight buds of her nipples.

Reece knelt to the ground, Lacy's legs still draped around him. He eased her onto soft spring grass shrouded conveniently by a hedge of honeysuckle. The yellow blooms teemed with scores of bees, a quiet hum droning in the background as the sweet scent filled their lungs, and her sweet mouth and soft body made every inch of him rigid with need.

Nimble fingers fumbled with the buttons of his shirt. He wanted nothing else than to strip naked and bury himself inside her, but the fact that she was Thad's baby sister continued to scream at him through the fog of lust permeating his body.

"Lacy. What are you doing?" He stilled her hand and he met her questioning gaze. "We can't do this."

Her eyes sharpened with annoyance. Delicate fingers fanned across the top of his chest beneath his shirt and through the hairs of his chest as she watched his reaction with rapt attention.

Reece drew in a ragged breath, damning the surge of blood to his groin as he fought to maintain control.

"Tell me you don't want me to," she breathed against his chin. "Tell me you don't want this as much as I do, Reece."

He gazed into the depths of her chocolate eyes. Eyes that invited him to plunder her spoils at will. Eyes he wanted nothing more than to lose himself in.

Dear Lord. He had no willpower. He was lost to Lacy Wills, consequences be damned.

Reece captured the plush softness of her lips, nipping and suckling the pliable sweetness of her lower lip. Sweet murmurs escaped her throat as those fingers worked against the resistance of wet fabric to loosen each remaining button, until her warm palms traced the flat planes of his lower abdomen and moved to his back. He arched against the tender rake of her nails, then rolled carefully to press his groin into the space between her thighs.

"Oh, Lacy." Propping himself on his elbows, Reece held her head and shoulders between his arms.

She loosed her hair and smiled up at him, her curls a spray of chestnut against the grass. Sunlight dappled her freckle-dusted cheeks. Reece's heart clenched tight in his chest. She was beautiful.

Such unabashed innocence and perfect trust. How could he take advantage of her?

Lacy worked her arms under his chest, and her fingers pulled at the buttons on her own shirt. Reece's brain told him to make her stop, but his mouth refused to form the words. He followed each movement as she exposed section after tiny section of creamy skin.

"Lacy, it shouldn't be like this." He wrapped her hands in his to halt her progress, but then faltered.

Her eyes smoldered as she smoothed the edges of the cotton shirt past the swell of each breast. She loosened the ties of her chemise in a flash. Her dusky, taut peaks beguiled him. Reece moaned low and rolled to his side, curling his leg over one of hers as his hand traveled over the smooth dips of her belly and along the curve of her waist.

She felt like silk. His hand engulfed the full measure of one breast. At the slightest squeeze, her breath caught in her throat. He pressed the soft mound into his palm.

Good lord, the feel of her put him in paradise.

Reece found the temptation of her breast too much to bear. He glanced at her heavy-lidded eyes responding with pleasure and dipped his head to suckle one dark nipple, circling it with his tongue. He sucked it past the edge of his teeth and reveled in the way her body bucked gently against his. Her hand grabbed his shirt and she tensed.

His leg edged between hers, rubbing the curve of his knee into the juncture at her thighs. Lacy turned in toward the pressure and pressed her velvet lips to the hollow of his throat. Fire shot through him again, and Reece began to fear himself more than Thad's rage.

Nimble fingers worked the buttons of his trousers loose, and before he realized what was happening, she'd palmed his entire length. He sucked in a breath to steady himself as the blood rushed away from his brain. Another heated groan eased from his throat at the soft touch of her hand. She was heaven on earth, and he hadn't gotten as far as his body intended. Good Lord, if he ever took her, he'd probably die of pleasure right here.

"Oh, Reese." Lacy moaned as her hand began a heated stroke across his cock. "I never dreamed."

"Dreamed what, honey?" He planted kisses over the swell of each breast as his hands rubbed warmth along the curves from her hips to her breasts. She was exquisite.

"That you could be so large." Her fingers tightened around him and every muscle in his body tightened as she pulled up.

"Good Lord, Lace. Don't do that. You'll have me going off, and I'm not ready, not yet." He nuzzled the hollow of her neck, breathing in the scent that was wholly Lacy until her grip loosened.

Her hands moved from his cock to slip beneath the waist of his trousers. Each delicate hand trailed warmth over his rear as she worked the wet fabric off his behind and down his thighs.

She tipped her head up and grinned as the material cleared his knees. With some effort, he worked off his boots and socks and kicked the pants loose, shedding the shirt in the process before his fingers found the buttons of her trousers. It was almost a fight between them who could loosen the darned little fasteners the quickest. Lacy almost had them torn from the fabric before she tugged at the canvas and her drawers to expose the triangle of dark curls at the apex of her slender thighs.

Reece's mouth went dry as he took her in, all of her. She lay on the green mound of grass, propped on her slender elbows, eying him expectantly. Trust widened her brown eyes. He leaned over her, supporting himself on extended arms. Thad would kill him for what he wanted to do with Lacy. His brain told him back away, but Lacy reached up and pulled him down.

Her tug was insistent and demanding. He couldn't deny her.

Dear Lord, he didn't want to deny himself. A burning hunger engulfed him.

Reece lowered his body over Lacy's. Skin against skin, his blood boiled and his heart hammered. He couldn't breathe for the sheer joy of touching Lacy Wills, all of her. Her breasts pressed hot, soft circles against his chest. Her thighs moved against his rough hair. Lacy moaned against the heat of his skin. Any stray droplets of water between them seemed to sizzle at the contact.

His body pressed her cautiously into the soft grass beneath them. She shifted her thigh, opening herself up to him. Reece stopped breathing altogether when he felt her slender leg slide up the outside of his thigh and over his buttocks. His cock nestled against the soft hairs at her groin. The contact made tension spiral through him. He didn't see how he could last. Lacy beneath him and around him. He really had died and gone to heaven.

Lacy's arms circled his neck. Her hands grabbed fistfuls of hair as her supple lips brushed kisses up his throat and along his jaw before laying claim to his mouth. The pounding of his heart against his ribs paled only in comparison to the heavy throb in his cock.

Take it slow, he reminded himself. Reece didn't want to rush her. "Are you sure about this?" He muttered between kisses.

Her brown eyes gazed up at him. Longing and desire warmed them—the same longing he'd held in for the past year. It surfaced with such vigor he prayed she wouldn't ask him to restrain it.

"More sure than anything in my life, Reece McCord."

Her pelvis angled against him, pushing against his hard length. He sucked in a breath to settle the raging inferno inside him. Supporting himself on one elbow, Reece slid one hip to the grass and eased one hand down her flat belly, reveling in the silky feel of her skin. His hand found that sweet place between her thighs. He felt her stiffen at his touch.

Leaning forward, his lips brushed a tender kiss on her brow. "It's okay, honey. Just relax."

"I'm not afraid with you, Reece." Lacy's pink mouth turned up at the edges as she pressed into his palm. "Touch all of me, please."

"I could kiss all of you, darlin'."

"Mmm. That would be nice too." Those brown eyes of hers slid shut, and her body writhed under him.

His heart took to flight. She wanted him. Lacy Wills wanted him. At that moment Reece felt his heart soar. He wanted her for his own. He wanted Lacy as his only. If she would have him, he'd move the moon for her.

Reece's hand slid between her folds to lay his claim. A groan erupted from his throat. Moisture wet his hand as one finger slid inside her. She arched against his touch while her fingers dug delicious pressure points into his shoulders. Desire coated her voice as tender moans invited deeper exploration. Lacy instinctively widened her thighs for easier access.

Oh Lord. He could have her in an instant, as hard and aching as he was. But what pleasure would she have in that? Reece wanted her to revel in the gift as well as the giving. Easy was the way to go with his beauty.

His hand began a gentle thrusting as his thumb pressed into her tiny nub of pleasure. The contact with her clit drove her into his hand and elicited an exquisite squeal of pleasure on Lacy's part. Good God, the thrill that sound gave him.

"You have to do more, Reece. I need more."

"Easy, Lace. You don't want me to rush it, do you?"

"Yes! Oh please, I need all of you."

Reese eased in another finger, applying more pressure to

stretch her wider. To his relief, her body responded warmly, relaxing at his touch.

"I mean now, or I'll do it myself."

Reece suppressed a roll of laughter. "I can't refuse you anything."

He rolled on top of her, his elbows supporting most of his weight on either side of her slight body. Reece watched her with uncertainty. He barely breeched her, pausing to halt his intrusion into her sweet body should she change her mind. She moved into him in invitation. Lacy didn't close her eyes or hide the awe of the moment from him. Her wide eyes took him in, urging him on in wordless wonder.

Lacy's legs crawled up his hip and hooked behind his back. She locked her ankles and tightened her grip on him.

With one easy thrust, he slid inside her. Warmth and moisture engulfed him in an envelope of intense pleasure. If he wasn't already on his knees, the ecstasy of Lacy around him would have brought him there. A steady throb of tension coiled from his lower back to his balls as he began languorous thrusts to sate his unquenchable thirst for Lacy.

Lacy clung to him, meeting every thrust and sway with her body. If he hurt her, she never showed it. She writhed beneath him, inciting a surge of heat and desire the likes of which Reece had never before known with any other woman.

Her body tightened around him, revealing the depths of a desire as deep and fathomless as his. Reese growled deep in his throat as he moved within her, grinding his hips tight against her supple body. The wonderful, feminine sounds erupting quietly from Lacy's graceful throat drove him closer to release. The pull of her legs around his back and the constant dig of her fingers into his flesh brought him nearer the edge.

In a moment Lacy climaxed and a quiet scream erupted from

her lungs. Her body clenched around him, pulsing and throbbing. One more thrust and Reese felt his world explode as his release surged through him. His grasp on her tightened, pulling her closer into him. He breathed in the scent of clean Lacy and grass as his body tightened as rigid as a board.

The intimate joining of their bodies melded Lacy to his heart and soul. She was his. He just prayed she wouldn't give him any guff about it. Lacy Wills was all he ever wanted of this life.

It took a few minutes for his body to relax and come down from the pinnacle to which Lacy had taken him. Reece rolled off her, nestling beside her, one arm draped across her middle and his head resting on the other arm. He could spend all his days touching this beautiful woman. Caring for and making her happy was all he needed.

Lacy stretched beside him. Her hand rubbed a warm trail up his arm as she nudged a shoulder into his chest. Her eyes fluttered half-open, giving her a dreamy look. A smile the size of Texas graced her lush mouth. "That was...that was so incredible. Reece McCord, I had no idea."

"That was pretty darned wonderful, darlin'." His hand rubbed lazy circles over her belly. "I never felt like this before, Lacy."

"Was this your first time, too?" Her eyes took him in with incredulity.

"No, honey. I mean this is the first time I've made love. Those other times didn't mean anything like this." Reece worked the muscles of his throat. His free hand encased the side of her face. "I love you, Lacy Wills. I want you in my bed every night and every morning. And if your brother ever gets wind of this, he'll kill me. So you better tell me you'll marry me now. I really don't want a shotgun wedding any more than you do."

Lacy pushed against his chest. "What makes you so sure I

want to marry you, Reece? There's plenty of good ol' boys interested in me."

"That may be true. But you aren't in love with any of 'em.
You're in love with me, Lacy Wills. There isn't anything you can
say to make me believe otherwise."

A delicate rosy hue colored her cheeks. She couldn't hide the
truth from him. He knew her too well.

"I don't want a shotgun wedding. I guess you have me in a
spot. I'll have to marry you, Reece McCord."

He wrapped his arms around her and pressed her close.
She'd caught him unawares. It made him the happiest man in
the world.

SOME LIKE
IT DIRTY

Kimber Vale

Jenna McManus stood on the side of the road and kicked the tire of her Lexus RX Hybrid with a filthy Lanvin heel. The crystal flower perched atop the pricey platform pump was already coated with a layer of grime that made it unrecognizable. The tune to "Rhinestone Cowboy" popped into her head as she grimaced at her ruined footwear. It only made her angrier.

"How anyone can live in these conditions is beyond me!"

She was talking to herself in the middle of a deserted stretch of Oklahoma road. *Well, not completely deserted.*

Off in the distance, a cluster of black and white cows milled about, grazing for green tufts of grass in the scorching afternoon sun.

"Dammit! I knew I never should have gotten an electric car!" Jenna struck the offending piece of tin once more, this time with a fist. The clunk of flesh against the metal roof seemed to reverberate, echoing in a rhythmic beat, until she recognized the sound. Pounding hooves thundered in the distance. She shaded her eyes with an aching hand and turned to see a man on horse-back. He sat tall on his massive animal and was accompanied by a lightning-fast blur of a dog, whirling around the bovines and whipping them into a tidy bunch.

Jenna took a final look at her cell phone.

Great, still no reception.

With a huff of resignation, she flounced off across the dry earth, her heels sinking lower than her heart. This trip was turning out to be a trillion times worse than anticipated. Waving her hands over her head, she saw the cowboy take notice and turn his mount in her direction.

Thank God. There must be a land line around here some-where.

It was unreal that her company, Natural You, had sent her to bum-fuck nowhere to scout out one of their organic milk suppliers for ad campaign potential.

What potential?

This place was a wasteland. The company would do better to build an entire set and hire people to dance around in cow costumes. Sure, the public loved the idea of natural and organic products, but generally speaking, they weren't all that into nature. It was disgusting and dirty when you got up close to it.

"Shit!" She stepped in a cow pie. If the shoes weren't garbage before, they certainly were now. Maybe she could expense them.

The stranger galloped toward her at a nerve-jangling clip. The dog—black, white, and furry—streaked along at his side. Between man, horse, and hound, she imagined being mowed down. No wonder the cows were so compliant. The threesome was fearsome.

He reined in next to her amid a swirl of floating dust. Jenna stepped back and landed her other shoe in the same pile of cow crap. The dog sat, wagging a friendly tail and almost smiling. Jenna gazed up at the face under the ten-gallon hat. The eyes were shadowed, his image backlit by the afternoon sun, so she was unable to make out his features. But she could swear he was grinning as well.

"Better watch your step, there, miss. This is no place for fancy shoes."

He swung off his saddle; on foot, he still towered nearly a foot over her head—even with her four-inch heels. She could see his face now: tan, with generous lips that quirked up in an ironic half-smile. His blue eyes crinkled at the corners as he gazed down at her dirty feet. His entire body seemed to be coated in a layer of filth. His blue jeans were smeared with brown handprints. His once-white T-shirt was now a shade of tan, with yellow patches under the arms from a full day's sweat. It hugged his chiseled chest, leaving Jenna's mouth even drier than the eighty-degree weather demanded. She swallowed—or tried to—and cleared her throat.

She held a hand out to shake his gritty one. It was warm and powerful, despite the dirt. "Hi. Thanks for coming over to help. I desperately need to get to a phone. I have a meeting to cancel and a tow truck to call. Stupid hybrid car."

He stared at her in silence as if trying to translate her foreign language.

"God forbid you guys actually have cell reception out here! A person could die stranded on this stretch of road." She smiled, hoping to reel him into the conversation. "I can't believe they actually call this piece of asphalt an interstate. It's barely a step above a goat trail."

The cowboy raised an eyebrow, but the slight smile remained on his delicious mouth. It looked more challenging than sympathetic. She was totally bungling this.

"I'll give you a ride to my ranch so you can make your calls."
He held the reins of his dark brown, obviously male horse, and
gestured for her to climb up.

"What? I can't ride on that thing. This is a knee-length pencil
skirt. It doesn't do horses." It was a Burberry, but she spared
this guy the brand name; she doubted he knew any tags beyond
Hanes and Levi's.

Her eyes skimmed down his jean-clad legs. Scuffed brown
boots stepped directly in front of her.

"I'll just walk," she said, wondering why he was suddenly
in her personal space. She could smell him now; he emanated a
musky scent born of sweat and soil. A fine blend of animal and
man—or maybe it was all animal. Something about this guy
was decidedly undomesticated.

His rough palms landed on her hips, grazing her ass as they
worked down the sides of her tight skirt.

"What are you doing?"

She hated how her voice sounded breathless, how her nipples
were poking through the thin silk of her blouse in response to
his touch. She wanted to sound angry instead of aroused. Major
fail.

"Just lending a helpin' hand to a damsel in distress," he
growled as the sound of tearing fabric startled her out of her
unbidden fantasy. The warm breeze that blew across the prairie
was suddenly caressing the flesh of her exposed buttocks. Jenna
reached a fearful hand back to grasp a bare cheek. The two-inch
slit in her three-hundred-dollar garment had grown exponen-
tially.

"Up you go," he said, stepping behind her and lifting her
under the arms as if she were a newborn calf. He tossed her into
the saddle, the leather warm and supple between her legs. The
crotch of her silk thong was a token barrier between her naked

skin and the butter-soft hide. The skirt was hiked up around her hips, betraying the garter that held up her silk hose. Jenna was certain her ass was on display for the stranger.

"What the hell are you thinking?"

She tried to sound authoritative. Outraged. Where was the Jenna from the boardroom meetings—the woman who drove fear into the hearts of new hires and old-timers alike? Somehow, unthinkably, her voice came out squeaky and panicked. The dirt-streaked cowboy stuck a boot tip in a stirrup and swung up behind her.

Her crotch was pushed forward, grinding responsive nerve endings against the unyielding saddle horn. She felt his chest, warm granite against her back, as his arms encircled her to coax the stallion into a rolling canter. Jenna couldn't ignore the sensation of his legs wrapped around hers. His thick, denim-encased manhood was pressed against her bare ass. It surged against her with each jarring step. Her pussy was getting wet from the dual sensations of being sandwiched between hard leather and hard man.

He destroyed your clothing without so much as a "pardon me." He's more animal than man. Stop getting turned on by the brute!

But that was easier thought than done. That sliver of feral beast was an incredible turn on. The longer they rode—his burnished forearms brushing against her erect nipples as he pulled on the reins—the hotter Jenna became. She could almost swear the size of the hard bulge snug against her thong was growing bigger with each bounce. Without conscious thought, she wiggled against his cock and was rewarded with a low groan that rumbled in her ear.

A log house materialized in the distance. Actually, the term house didn't do the place justice. It was a sprawling compound, backed by a massive barn and a spacious fenced-in area full of cows.

"Wow. Is this your place?"

"Always belonged to my family, but my sister got married and moved to Texas. I'm the last one keepin' up with it. My folks have been gone for a number of years now."

She loved the sound of his drawl, she realized suddenly. Low and soulful, sweet and Southern; it made her think of Elvis and molasses. Or maybe Elvis covered in molasses. No one in California spoke like that; she could almost guarantee it.

"Phone's in the kitchen, straight on through. Feel free to make your calls and get fixed up."

He heaved her off of the seat and the cool air that met her naked backside was disappointing after his warm cocoon. She turned to see him grinning as he looked over her exposed skin. If he wasn't still up on that horse she'd like to slap him. Or perhaps kiss him.

Definitely both.

"I gotta go pick up those stragglers I left out there. Be right back." He spun the horse around and galloped off in a riot of hammering hooves and billows of brown.

"Wonderful," she spat at his retreating form. "I'll go find your sewing kit and make myself presentable for my meeting with the head of the Remington Dairy Corporation. Better yet, I'll just stay like this and hope he has a splendid sense of humor and an eye for a round ass. Might make our business negotiations run more smoothly."

The front door was unlocked, and Jenna kicked off her revolting heels before stepping into the rustic yet elegantly furnished home. It was amazingly tidy. Not at all what she'd imagined. The décor was masculine and modern, with clean lines and a simplicity that bordered on Spartan. Somehow, it managed to be both chic and warmly inviting at the same time. The natural wood and comfortable earth-toned fabrics created a beautiful and relaxing space.

She had wondered whether or not there was a Mrs. Cowboy, but not anymore. This place screamed testosterone.

The kitchen was modern and streamlined; the phone easy to find on the spotless black countertop. Jenna dug her cell out of her clutch and scrolled through to the number for Mr. Trent Remington. She got his voicemail and left a brief message asking to reschedule on account of car trouble. Her trip into rodeo hell would be delayed at least one extra day by this major inconvenience.

Next, she called her secretary in L.A. and asked the dutiful woman to send a tow truck for the rental lemon. Originally, the notion of a "green" vehicle had appealed to her. Mr. Remington was known to be a zealous tree-hugger and a little ass-kissing had never hurt her career.

Whatever. She wouldn't repeat the gesture. Tomorrow, she would show up for their meeting in a tried-and-true gas guzzler. At least traditional cars had been around long enough to iron out all of the bugs.

Wandering around the lower level, Jenna found a living area, a killer media room, and a huge four-season porch that would probably showcase a gorgeous sunset. She stood before the two-story window, watching the first pink and orange wisps of color paint the horizon. For a moment she could understand the allure of rural life. The view was sublime.

The touch on her back caused her to jump, and she spun around to face her grungy rescuer—only now he was clean. His towel-dried hair stood up in erratic waves of sun-tipped chocolate brown. A day or two of stubble still darkened his sculpted cheeks and strong chin, but he had changed into a fresh pair of jeans. The cowboy had neglected to put on anything else.

His tawny chest was chiseled, with a fine layer of gilded hair sprinkled across his substantial pectorals. She looked down at his sockless feet and realized that even they were attractive, tanned. Oddly sexy.

"You've got quite a view here." She knew how it came out; knew she was staring at his amazing body and licking her lips.

"I was thinkin' the same thing when I walked in."

Jenna glanced up to see the sly smile on his face. Up close, she noticed the dimples that showcased his gorgeous grin. Shit. She was a sucker for dimples. Then his words sank in—she'd forgotten that her ass was still bare and exposed.

"This is an expensive skirt, I'll have you know."

"I'll buy you a new one. You couldn't have walked all the way here in your city-girl shoes."

She took a deep breath for a scathing retort, but his hands stopped her. They were on her waist once more, sliding toward her backside. He smelled of soap, with an underlying virile essence a thousand showers could never wash away. His natural male scent had her head spinning and her hormones raging in response. It was like he was the alpha of his species, pheromones and all, and she was helpless against his allure.

"I s'pose I could've taken it off instead." His nimble fingers found her zipper and slid it down with unbearable indolence. The fabric fell around her feet, leaving nothing but thin silk and lacey underclothes between his searing gaze and her trembling body. Suddenly that barrier felt too oppressive.

"Why stop there?" She unbuttoned her blouse as she spoke, enjoying the hungry gleam in his swimming-pool eyes as he followed her every move. "You could have draped me across your saddle buck-naked like some prisoner you were taking back to your hideout."

His tongue moved greedily over his luscious lips. Jenna arched her back, thrusting pert nipples at him as she unclasped her bra and slid it off, dropping it on the floor.

"So now that you have me here, sir, what *will* you do with me?"

Faster than a striking rattler, his hand shot out and pulled her against him. His hungry mouth covered her lips, ravishing them inside and out. Rough stubble scratched against her cheeks as he kissed her deeply, twining his tongue with her own.

Jenna moaned, sucking on his lower lip. He had his hands in her hair, tipping her head back to blaze a trail of kisses across her jaw and down her neck. Teasing with his sandpaper skin, he nibbled at her shoulder blade. God, she wanted to feel that rough sensation tantalizing her breasts.

As if he could see into her mind, his head bent, and his hot mouth worked down to her chest, brushing agonizing bristles against her throbbing nipple before finally drawing it into his fiery mouth. He suckled her hard, flicking the tip with his tongue. Jenna cried out, thrusting against him before he moved to her other aching tit. All the while his hand toyed with the opposite nipple. He brushed the rigid peak with a thumb, weighing her B-cup in his palm like the two were puzzle pieces long separated and finally united for a perfect fit.

Unexpectedly, Jenna felt him shift his bulk; his massive arms swept her off her feet in a fluid motion. She wrapped her arms around his neck, feeling disconcertedly helpless. Her whole life was about control and power. This man was ripping the rug right out from under her, but the vulnerability she was experiencing with her cowboy was bizarrely stimulating. Erotic beyond imagining.

"I prefer to take my prisoners in the bedroom. I'm old-fashioned that way."

That deep baritone rolled through his chest, setting off sparks across her naked breasts as they pressed against him. Before she knew it, she was tossed lightly on a massive bed and looking up at the most handsome man she had ever been with. His gaze was smoldering as he unzipped his Levis and let them fall. Next, he lost his form-hugging boxer-briefs to stand before her like a Greek statue made of magnificent flesh.

His cock stood straight, a divining rod pointed in her direction. It was thick and long, utterly appetizing, but her perusal was brief. He lowered his body, the quads in his legs rippling while his warm, rough hands slid up her calves. Up her thighs. His fingers found the band of elastic that made up her thong. With sensual ease, he peeled off her thong and stockings, discarding every last stitch of her overpriced clothing.

His masterful hands kneaded the soft skin between her thighs, teasing upward toward her tormented pussy while her belly pulsed with anticipation. His eyes were locked on hers all the while, calculating her reaction, making sure his touch had the desired effect. Finally, the tips of his fingers skimmed across her smooth lips.

Jenna's breath was shallow, an expectant pant like a wounded animal waiting for the final blow. It came in the form of a slow, deliberate finger that slipped inside her moist slit. He teased at her hole, barely sliding inside her, lubricating his fingertip to glide back up to her clit.

He swirled her pleasure point expertly until she was gasping. His eyes were stormy, dark with desire as his head dipped toward her cunt. Two fingers slid inside her, and his tongue took up where they left off. It flicked her mercilessly while his calloused fingers fucked her in time. He took her hard nub inside his mouth, sucking her like a demon, while his prickly cheeks teased her lips. Jenna's body stiffened under him. She cried out as she came, grabbing his thick mane of hair as the waves of a tremendous orgasm swept over her.

The cowboy moved up her body. His lips found hers, his tongue tasting like her most private space and driving her mad with desire. Jenna felt his steely tip nudge against her still-throbbing flesh, felt him push against her tight hole. He entered her in a thrust while the lingering crests still took her. Filled with his huge cock, she bit his shoulder as he ground against her clit. He pushed balls-deep inside her and nudged her orgasm on and on. He stroked in and out of her dripping pussy, picking up speed in time with her pitching hips.

"You're so wet...so hot." Lips against her ear, he murmured his pleasure in warm bursts of air, nipping at her lobe as he rocked between her legs.

He moved back, sitting up on his knees and grasping her ankles. Her calves rested against his muscular chest, and he pulled his cock out of her to run his bulging head up and down the slick crease. His sensitive tip rubbed against her until she couldn't stand another moment of the exquisite torture.

"Put it in me, cowboy. I need you right now."

He obliged by working his helmet in between her lips ever so slowly, fucking her with just his tip while his thumb worked her clitoris.

She wanted to scream. Or come. He read her signals and rammed deep inside her, fucking her hard and fast to the rhythm of his frenzied thumb. Jenna did both. She cried out in exquisite release, clamping down on his meat with a vise-like grip. His head tossed back, he sounded his own climax in an animal growl. His cock bucked inside her as he came in a hot rush. Falling back down, he covered her mouth with greedy kisses. The lingering taste of her juice on his lips was like a sweet drug and Jenna closed her eyes, losing herself in blissful serenity.

She woke up in the dark room, naked but for a sheet. Wrapping the cotton around her body, she struck out to find the man who had rocked her world a short while ago. How could she have just fallen asleep like that? Guess it had been a while since she'd gotten off so thoroughly and fantastically. A mind-blowing fuck could be exhausting.

A mouth-watering odor beckoned her toward the kitchen. Mr. Levi's was just putting a fabulous spread on the table.

"Free-range roast duck with new potatoes and fresh garden greens. I would've taken you out, but you're hardly dressed for it." He grinned down at her, crinkling eyes and deep dimples melting her on the spot as he swept her into his arms and placed a light kiss on her lips. "Sure hope you don't show up for all your business meetings in your birthday suit, Jenna."

She froze as her stomach dropped about thirty floors. Her gaze met his, willing him to explain what she already knew.

"Trent Remington, at your service, miss. I got your phone message while you were asleep. I'm more than happy to postpone the business end of things until tomorrow, and we can just enjoy each other's company this evenin'."

His smile was heart-stopping. Jenna felt her body beginning to respond to his nearness. For once she didn't know what to say. It wasn't like he could be blamed for fooling her. She hadn't even asked his name.

"Well, this trip is certainly looking up." She gave him a coquettish grin as she reached up to plant another kiss on those killer lips. Warm arms circled her protectively as she molded her body against her cowboy. Getting dirty had never been so much fun.

Jenna couldn't wait to do it again.

RANEY'S
LAST RIDE

Chaparrita

Raney James had a big secret.

He was a gunslinger, a lover, a mystery. A badass in chaps and a white cowboy hat. Charming and fresh-faced, with deep green eyes that made people trust him straight away. Something that made you want to look twice—except Raney didn't allow that. No, sir.

Raney was the fastest shot in the territory, a vicious yet fair gunman who'd always let his opponent know before killing him. *Give a man fair warning*, Raney would say. *Then shoot him if he won't listen.*

He rode in from the west one day, an unknown, making his way to the dusty border towns where saloons, wranglers, and gun work were plentiful. Raney made his name as sheriff of a forlorn place that barely had a railroad station, a place where local outlaws had taken over and would shoot someone in the back just for looking at them funny.

One afternoon on the main street, in front of most of the

good citizens of the town, Raney shot all four outlaw leaders before even one could draw a weapon. Their men left town without looking back.

No one was really close to Raney except his sidekick Whitfield, a tough erstwhile cowboy and gunman who'd taken up with Raney somewhere in Mexico.

Only Whitfield knew Raney's big secret.

Raney James, fastest shot in the territory, was a *woman*.

Once upon a time, Raney was a rancher's wife named Sarah. She married Paul on a perfect spring day in a white dress, a crown of pink roses in her long blonde hair. She remembered Paul's brown eyes shining as the preacher said the solemn words. The green of the fields. How proud her parents looked. Nineteen years old.

When Paul was courting her, they'd spent a few evenings lying on a quilt in his field, talking as the sun went down in a blaze of tangerine. And once it was down, the shining stars covered them as they kissed, Paul's urgent caresses setting her on fire and his sinful words laying her bare.

The wedding night with her husband, though, was pure revelation, something she was unprepared for. On the four-poster bed he'd made for her, in the quiet after the long wedding day, he helped unwind the ribbons of her simple dress, and then sat and watched her hotly as she peeled off her clothes.

"I'm going to make you feel good, Sarah," Paul said, running his big, rough hand up the tender inside of her leg from heel to thigh.

She felt herself melting, blushing and curious in her nakedness. His hand lingered.

"This is going to be wild," he said. "I'm not going to take it easy on you. Is that all right with you, wife?"

"Yes, husband," she said.

And so he pulled her to him by her hips, and tasted her breasts ravenously as his hands traveled up and down her arms and belly.

The moment his mouth met her nipple, an electric shock ran down to her pussy. She drew a sharp breath, not knowing how to handle the powerful feelings. She decided the best course was to surrender and let him do whatever he wanted with her body.

He coaxed every inch of her to life with his fingers, mouth, and tongue, and along the way taught her words for body parts, words that were new to her. Cock. Pussy. Cunt. Ass. "My woman will be a lady on the ranch and a spitfire in the boudoir," he said. As liquid seeped down her leg, he moved on top of her and pushed his hard cock inside with a moan.

It was the most wonderful thing she'd ever felt in her life.

Later, he would teach her how to take his cock into her mouth, how to suckle and grip the hard shaft until he came in a furious gush. She wondered where men learned these things. She didn't care. She wanted more.

On their wedding night, he rode her body for miles. Took her from above, below, behind, as roughly as she'd seen bulls mounting mares in the pasture. When they were done, he held her and murmured sweet nothings about how he loved her. And she was his. No other way to be, but his.

Love words weren't the only things he taught her. He also taught her fighting words, guns, and horses. "No woman of mine is going to be defenseless," he said, placing a Colt in her hands. Then she surprised him: she wasn't scared of it. She could hit a target cleanly, with one shot. Her father had also thought that women should know how to shoot—and shoot well—because he went out on long cattle drives, and she and her mom and brothers were often alone. It was just practical to teach them all. She'd never needed to use her skills. Her husband honed her ability, practicing with her almost every day, until her natural expertise and speed were razor-sharp. When they went out hunting, she was always the one to bring down the prey.

Sarah took the wagon into town one day to pick up supplies at the general store. Paul was no longer worried about her traveling on her own. "You're the best shot I've ever seen in my life," he said. "It's the bandits I'm worried about." He smiled. "Hurry home, wife. I want to eat your roast, and then get you into bed," he said, patting her—and then the horse Snowflake—on the rump.

In town, she took notice of other women. Fancy dresses. Lacy fans. They had to have men help them through doors and out of wagons, tumbling about in a helpless flounce of skirts. What would become of women without men? They'd either be whores or outcasts. Sarah felt the cool metal of the Colt strapped against her thigh and smiled. She would never be any of those things.

Coming home, she knew something was wrong as soon as she got within sight of the ranch. Things were too quiet: no sounds from the barn. Even the birds were silent. No cows were in the pasture. She nudged Snowflake's flank to go faster. When they reached the house, she saw the front door wide open, and yelled, "Paul?"

No answer. He *always* met her when she returned from town. She leapt from the wagon and ran into the house. On the kitchen table was a note, held down with one silver candlestick.

Sorry for your loss, ma'am. Didn't want to do it, but
he fought us too hard over the horses and cattle.
   Sincerely, Bill Jessup

The paper fluttered from her hands, and she ran to the back of
the house to their bedroom. Paul lay face down on the floor,
one gunshot wound to the back of the heart, leaking blood
onto the floor next to their marital bed.

Sarah screamed, kept on screaming, and sank to the wooden
floor with the crumpled note from the outlaw in her hands.

Bill Jessup, she thought. *Bill Jessup.* She committed every
detail to memory. *There will be no mercy when I find you, Bill
Jessup.*

The next morning, she buried her husband at sunup, in the
field where he'd once courted her. Set fire to the house and the
ranch to destroy all trace of who she had once been—for Sarah
had died with Paul. Raney James lived on, taking only her
horse and a saddlebag full of rations and bullets. She rode away
in her dead husband's clothing, her long blonde hair knotted
tightly under his white cowboy hat.

Raney became tougher, determined not to become one of the
outcast women she used to pity. Became tough so she would
survive long enough to find and kill Bill Jessup. It was a lonely
road. Sometimes in her hotel room above a saloon in some
random town, she'd brush her long blonde hair in front of a
mirror and cry for the love she'd had with Paul. The simplicity
of her old life.

One town began to look like the next. Her days ran
together.

Raney took lovers over the years. She found herself needing
the release of a hard fuck after a long day of gunslinging. Her

favorite had been a rough young man who somehow intuited her unladylike needs. During the day, he posed as her saddle boy. At night, they'd find a discreet place to tear into each other. One night, they had to go into the hills to get far enough away from the dusty little town in which they'd found themselves.

She jumped off her horse, and he immediately pressed his mouth against hers, the dirt from their faces smudging together, his tongue greedy. He ripped off her hat, letting her long blonde hair tumble out the way he liked it, and threw his sleeping bag down on a soft spot of grass and sand. The sky was a deep blue with streaks of dark orange where the sun had been. Coyotes howled. He unzipped his breeches, and before Raney could undo one button, he was fucking her mouth, his thick cock deep in her throat and his hands wrapped in her hair.

Man's work gave her a man's appetite, and she took his cock eagerly and gratefully, whimpering whenever he moved. She grasped his dick firmly, beating it along the shaft and swirling her mouth and tongue against his hardness until he groaned, and she felt his ass quivering under her fingers. She backed off.

"Hey," he growled, pushing her head right back on. And it was so good, she sucked him another minute more, relishing the salty taste of him, his girth brushing her lips. Then she felt him building up again and stopped.

"I want to feel this cock in my pussy," she said, smiling. *A spitfire in the boudoir.* The rough man obliged, moving to fuck her from behind, his balls smacking into her as she arched her back to take as much of him as possible, his hands eagerly holding her white, round hips. The hips that were usually hidden under her baggy man's breeches.

She liked this man for the raw, unashamed way he took her, continued taking her, opening her, fucking her. He made her forget, in brutal moments of sensation.

His fingers were on her clit, stroking her tenderly, bringing her to the edge and then over it. She cried out, felt his cock grow even harder, and smacked her hand into the dirt and said "Don't...stop."

He pulled out and spilled his seed on her back, grasping her hips as he slowed.

They fell asleep curled together under the violet sky and a full moon. There was tenderness between them. Nothing Raney would call love, but a sweet and dark understanding.

Which made it difficult, later. After some months the rough young man became territorial, wanting to push her around, acting like he owned her. When she said she didn't love him, he was enraged.

"Stop pretending to be a man and marry me," he said. "I'm man enough for both of us." He wasn't, though, and when he threatened to expose her to the world, drawing his loaded weapon on her, she shot him.

After that, she didn't risk any more love affairs. It had been two long and frustrating years since she'd been with anyone. She had tracked Bill Jessup to Mexico, only to have him evade her once again. But there, in a dark cantina, she met Whitfield. A quiet, strong, sure-shooting man. A man whose only interest was in killing Bill Jessup.

They sat together at the bar, not talking to anyone else, as was their way. Around them, whores mingled with the saloon patrons, and yells erupted from the card tables when someone raked in the chips. A blue haze of cigar smoke hung in the air.

Whitfield watched the back door while Raney watched the front. To the casual observer, they were preoccupied, sipping their whiskeys. Maybe even a bit drunk. But to the bartender, who had likely seen his share of violence, they were *watching*.

"Looking for someone?" he asked Whitfield, topping off the whiskey.

Whitfield didn't look at him. "Nope. Just looking," he said.

The bartender nodded.

Whitfield leaned towards Raney and quietly said, "That man told me Bill Jessup was riding in today. I paid the son of a bitch fifty dollars for the information."

Raney clapped him on the shoulder, to console him. Whitfield's wife had gotten caught in the crossfire during a robbery Bill's gang had perpetrated. Whitfield had helped her track the outlaw for a while now. He kept her secrets, and she trusted him completely.

The doors swung open and a good-looking tall man in a black hat entered. He had a long mustache and bright blue eyes. Two men came in with him. The whores chattered like a flock of birds, eyeing the new prey and preening themselves in their colorful dresses: red, pink, yellow. The patrons of the saloon, roughnecks and pretty boys alike, grew silent.

The tall man ambled right over to Raney, cutting through the crowd like a blade.

"Raney James," he said, his voice overly friendly. "I'd love to buy you a drink. I hear you're the one who took down Tom Parker in Brush City." He took a seat beside Raney and leaned back, resting his head in his interlaced fingers. "And I hear you might be the man who can beat me in a shootout."

Whitfield kept his gaze on the outlaw's men. Two beefy brutes, one blond, the other dark.

Raney gave him a steady nod. "I'd love some fine scotch. They don't pay the law much around here."

The tall man laughed. "So you're the law now? Well, let's drink to friendly relations."

They clinked glasses, and Raney never took her eyes off

him. She'd already pinpointed his weapons. One under the coat. One strapped to his leg. One on his belt. About the same places she carried her own firearms. Which he'd probably noticed, as well.

"What's a fella like you doing in a shithole like this?" Raney asked, taking a long draw on her scotch.

He laughed. "Same thing you are. Killing time." His eyes narrowed a fraction. "Care to make it more interesting with a little wager, Raney James? See who really is the better shot?"

Raney gave him a small smile. But only a small one. "I love when things get interesting, Bill Jessup."

The next morning at sunup, Whitfield and Raney left to meet Bill about thirty minutes outside of town. She was on Snowflake, and Whitfield rode the fine black stallion he called Mountain. The air was crisp and rarefied at that early hour, and the sky was clear. Bill and the two men he'd had with him at the saloon were sitting on rocks, poking at a dying fire, drinking coffee. "You always ride with only two men?" Raney asked, her hand on her gunbelt.

"Don't need more than that."

Then something went very wrong.

Joseph, as she'd learned the previous night, Bill's dark-haired man, took a shot at a coyote lurking nearby. Snowflake spooked, rearing hard and dumping Raney off her saddle. Jack, Bill's blonde man, managed to catch her, but it was a hard fall. And her hat fell to the ground, letting her long, pale hair loose. She gasped.

Whitfield immediately jumped off his horse to help her, but Bill put a gun to his back. "Well, look at this," Bill said.

"A woman?" Jack said, marveling at her hair, rubbing it between his fingers. "The great Raney James is a *woman?*" He took a handful of her ass. "This *is* a woman's ass."

Raney screamed and moved to punch Jack in the face.

Bill cocked his pistol and pushed it into Whitfield. "Calm down or I kill your man, here."

Bill and Joseph tied Whitfield up with rope and threw him to the ground. Jack put Raney down but kept his gun on Whitfield.

The outlaw strode over to Raney and grabbed her hair, whispering into her ear, "I always thought Raney James was a cocksucker. Turns out I was right." He and his men laughed.

She stared at him, not wavering, just waiting for the slightest chance to draw her Colt. Seething inside, but calm. Deadly calm. "What about the wager?" she said. "I want to shoot for our freedom."

"Deal," he said. "You win, we let you go. I win...you fuck me and my men." His eyes traveled greedily up and down her body, looking for the curves he now knew were under the clothes. "My word."

"Fine," she said tersely. "You have my word, too."

"Raney!" Whitfield called. "Just let them shoot me."

Bill shook her hand. "I'm going to fuck you first. In the mouth. Hard. Then Joseph will take you however he wants, which is probably up the ass, and I know Jack will want a piece of your sweet little gunfighting pussy." He paused and looked around. "We're going to put these two bottles of whiskey a hundred yards south. Let's see who breaks one first."

Jack ran out and positioned the bottles. Raney stood to the left and Bill to the right. Whitfield took a sharp breath. Jack said, "On the count of three."

And the bottle to the right shattered a split second before the one to the left. Whitfield yelled when he saw Raney's pale, blank face. Bill and his men whooped, jumping up and down, and Bill grabbed Raney around the waist. "You're fast—*for a woman*. But now it's time to pay up." He thrust his tongue down her throat, his mustache tickling her nose, kissing her until she felt warm. Then he tore her shirt open to reveal her pert, small breasts.

"Look at these fine tits, boys," he said, kneading them roughly. "And this ass," he said, undoing her pants harshly and pulling them down. He flipped her around and smacked her once, twice, reddening her white skin. He took her gunbelt off, tossing it to the side, and pulled the second gun off her leg. His men hooted and called for him to take her. Bill pushed Raney to her bare knees. "I can't wait to come in your mouth," he growled slowly, his voice giving away the depth of his need.

"I hate you," she said. But her anger fused with lust. Her body burned.

"I can live with that," Bill said.

Then he undid his own pants, pulling out a huge, thick erection.

She turned her head.

"Now open wide, Raney James," he said, turning her face to feed his full length in, holding the back of her head. He moaned as she began to suck, her hands instinctively coming up to hold the shaft as her mouth teased the tip.

Even though she hated Bill, his cock felt amazing, hard and wide, thrusting into the back of her throat. She was losing herself in it, letting herself be used. From the corner of her eye she saw Whitfield, staring at her transfixed. Jack held his gun in one hand, guarding Whitfield, and with the other he stroked his cock through his pants. His face was red, his mouth open in lust.

Joseph crouched on the ground about fifteen feet away, looking like he was about to pass out as he watched Raney take

Bill's cock. "Hurry up, boss," he groaned. "I need some of that real bad."

Bill didn't hurry. He took his time, opening her wide with his cock, fucking, pounding, murmuring appreciation and pushing his hips faster and faster into her face as she pulled his balls, and then felt his salty stream began to spurt into her throat, deep, hot, and strong. He continued to fuck until she'd taken every drop, then pulled away and sighed, zipping up.

Raney stood up and made a show of wiping her mouth off.

Bill walked away, smiling dreamily, and took Jack's spot guarding Whitfield. Jack moved so he could get a better view as Joseph positioned Raney on her knees. Joseph licked his hand a few times, wetting her with it, then nudged the head of his cock into her ass, testing, widening. She couldn't stop herself from moaning as he moved further and further inside her. The other men all moaned too, softly, without knowing it. Joseph was solid, with thick, hard thighs of rock, and his cock was the same.

With an animal grunt he pushed the whole of his dick into her, grasping her hips for traction, and fucked her slow, then fast. "You love this, don't you, you dirty little whore," he hissed. "Pretending to be a man, when you were just a filthy woman who wanted to get fucked like this."

She cried out in pleasure, and from the burn. Her eyes caught Whitfield's and held them as Joseph fed his dick into her over, over, and then came hard. She saw that Whitfield had an erection. Every man there was helpless with desire for her.

Jack laid a blanket on the ground and pulled her to it, gently. "I want to watch you suck this man's cock while I mount you," he said. Bill pushed Whitfield forward. Raney found she wanted this to happen.

Whitfield was shaking his head. "I don't fuck the boss," he said. "It's not right."

Bill said, "You will do it. Cause it's what Jack wants."

Jack positioned Raney on her hands and knees again, and she the heard the measured, metallic click of his zipper, felt the heat of his cock slipping into her.

"She acts like she don't want it, but her pussy is sopping wet," Jack moaned. *"She's in heat."* He held her breasts as he fucked her, and she felt herself climbing, the sensations radiating out from her cunt to every pore of her body.

Whitfield knelt in front of her and took out a beautiful cock, tall and proud, absolutely engorged. Silently, almost reverently he pushed himself into her mouth, stroking her hair. "That's real, real good," he murmured.

She had Jack in her pussy and Whitfield in her mouth, both men working her hard, working her right, and despite herself, the humiliation and the loss of her secret, the confusion, the thoughts of revenge, she came, not caring anymore, moaning her bliss around Whitfield. When he heard her, he cried out and shot into her mouth. She drank him down and felt Jack pull out as he climaxed loudly.

And then Whitfield picked her up, holding her to him, and kissed her full on the lips, a kiss full of tenderness and fire. Love, even. His hands held her face and he looked at her. And she at him, wonderingly. Seeing how he really felt. Then he narrowed his eyes and nodded imperceptibly. She winked.

It was time.

Raney's legs were shaky, and Bill brought her a canteen, from which she took a long, long drink. She got dressed, this time leaving her hair down under her white cowboy hat. She and Whitfield mounted their horses.

"Damn fine shooter and damn fine piece of ass," Jack said.

"I second that," said Bill. "Don't know about her being the fastest shot, though. I won." He smirked. "Now everyone's gonna know who Raney James really is."

Before anyone saw anything, Raney had her Colt out and shot a hole right through Bill's cowboy hat.

"Who said I didn't *let* you win?" she spat. "It seems you were the one who got screwed." Bill's face fell and his men drew their weapons. Raney shook her head in disbelief.

"You are a lousy shot, Bill Jessup," she said. "But you're a *marvelous* fuck."

Bill was furious. "I'm gonna kill you," he said.

Then Raney James shot him in the heart. For Paul.

Whitfield took out Bill's men, one after the other.

Raney and Whitfield nodded at each other, the landscape still ringing with the sudden shots.

"I love it when things get interesting," Whitfield said. And off they rode.

RUNAWAY BRIDE

Delilah Devlin

J ackson Lowry cussed softly when he spotted the blue lights
spinning at the roadblock just ahead. Too late to turn back
now. He'd only draw more attention.

Squaring his jaw, he rolled down his window and forced a
polite smile as he peered into the darkness at the sheriff's deputy
checking IDs with a flashlight.

As soon as the deputy waved the car in front of him to move
along and turned to watch the black pickup roll forward, Jackson's tension eased a fraction.

Maynard Colby's expression turned from crisply professional to worried in a second, as soon as he recognized Jackson.
"Dammit, Jackson, where have you been?"

"Around. Why?"

A soft moan sounded beside him, and Jackson reached
surreptitiously beside him to tap the tarp covering his precious
load.

"You didn't hear?" At Jackson's vague expression, Maynard

stepped onto the truck rail and leaned toward Jackson. "It's Sammi Jo. Her car was found in Shooter's parking lot, the door wide open. No one's seen her. Looks like she's been snatched."

Jackson cleared his throat. "How serious is this gettin'?"

"It's only been a couple of hours, but Sammi Jo's daddy is buckin' to get the sheriff to call in the FBI, the CIA, the ATF— and whatever other agency his money can buy to find her. I tried callin' you, but your phone kept goin' to voicemail. After the way things went down at the weddin' last Sunday, I don't blame you a bit for layin' low, but I thought you'd wanna know."

Another sound, this time a snort, sounded beside him.

Maynard's gaze cut to the dirty tarp folded over a moving bundle on the floor of the cab. A ruddy eyebrow shot up. "What's goin' on, Jackson?"

Jackson rolled his eyes, then pulled up the corner of the tarp to reveal a bound and gagged Sammi Jo whose eyes glittered furiously back at both men.

Maynard barked a laugh, then tightened his lips. "This time you've gone and done it, boy. This is seriously fucked up." He laughed again, then tipped his hat to Sammi Jo. "No disrespect meant, missy."

Jackson cleared his throat. "Don't s'pose you can forget about this?"

Maynard's gaze shot to Sammi Jo again, raked her once as though ensuring she didn't look to be in any real danger, then tipped back his cowboy hat. "Tell ya what. I'll put a bug in the sheriff's ear, but she better come walkin' through the *po*-lice house doors come Monday mornin'."

"Not a word to her daddy?"

One corner of Maynard's mouth crooked up. "Man's already caused enough problems. Deserves to cool his heels a couple o' days. Don't do nothin' I'll have to arrest you for."

With a nod, Jackson rolled up the window and pulled past the barricade. In his side mirror, he watched as Maynard crossed to the other deputy's car and both men bent over laughing.

"See that, Sammi Jo?" he murmured, not expecting an answer because he'd made double-damn sure he'd tied some serious knots and gagged her pretty mouth. "I'm not the only one who thinks you need a good paddlin'."

Sammi Jo Clements worked her jaw side to side to ease the ache. The dirty bandana was gone, but her mouth and tongue were swollen, and she was sure she had spit dried on her cheeks. The nerve of Jackson Lowry—kidnapping her in broad daylight!

And not a one of the customers lined up to peer out the saloon's windows had raised a hand to help or, apparently, to call the police. The fact that every one of them had kept mum about the whole thing burned a hole in her gut.

They all thought she'd been dead wrong—mean, even—to leave Jackson standing at the altar.

That had been only a couple of hours ago, but darkness had fallen swiftly. The cabin was awash in shadows that moved with the flicker of the gas lantern Jackson had hung from a hook in the ceiling.

A washcloth entered her view, and she snatched it from his hand to scrub her cheeks. "Don't know what you think you're gonna accomplish here. Daddy's gonna have your ass thrown in jail so fast you won't know what hit you."

Jackson grunted, then sat on the mattress beside her. He pulled down the brim of his hat and leaned back against the rough headboard as though he was getting ready to take a nap. "Daddy's got nothing to do with this," he drawled. "It's between you and me. Always has been. The fact you let him get to you—

well, that's just one of the things we're gonna discuss."

"Discuss?" She eyed the length of rope attached to her left arm. "This can only end badly—unless you drop me at home. I'll tell him I got drunk and decided to sleep in a ditch."

Jackson chuckled, a sound that never failed to make her nerves twitch. "With your reputation, he might believe it."

She tilted her chin and gave him a scalding stare. The truth hurt, but he didn't have to rub it in. So she'd been a party girl. So what? Jackson had known what he was getting into when he first asked her out. "No need to get snide."

"I don't wanna waste my breath tellin' you something you already know."

"Then what is it you want to *discuss?*" She wished like hell she could see his eyes, because they always reflected exactly what he thought, but the brim of his hat cast deep shadows.

His sexy mouth curved in a smile. "Maybe 'discuss' was just a euphemism."

"Huh?"

"Yeah," he said, his voice clipped now. "It's just something else you don't get." Jackson leaned forward to set his elbows on his thighs. His head dipped between his shoulders. Then he turned his face toward her and light glinted in his dark eyes. His gaze nailed her, sliding over her face, which she knew wore an expression as stubborn as a mule's. Then his hot stare trailed down the rest of her body.

Heat seeped into her cheeks. "That what this is all about? You think I owe you somethin'?" His huffing breath told her she'd guessed wrong and pissed him off, but she was too stubborn to take it back. She tilted her chin higher.

Jackson shook his head. "Sweetheart, you are some piece o' work. You think I brought you here to get what you promised?"

"Didn't you? What else am I supposed to think? You have me tied to a goddamn bed."

His snort this time seemed directed inward. He took off his hat and raked a hand through his short, dark hair. "Guess I wasn't thinkin' at all. I'd imagined you stretched across my bed so many times..." He pushed off the mattress, placed his hat on a crude wooden table, and then strode toward a grimy window. He stood there for a long moment with his back to her, staring out into the darkness so long she began to wonder if he was having second thoughts about what he'd done.

Sammi Jo was having second thoughts of her own—about whether she wanted him to let her go. He'd gone to a lot of trouble, risked arrest—or worse—to get her here. She was curious now about what he intended. "What is this place, anyway?"

"My family's huntin' cabin." He glanced over his shoulder and gave her another dark, unreadable stare. "Not up to your high standards?"

Lord, he didn't know her at all. Not that it was his fault. She'd led him on a merry chase, never letting him see her in any condition other than perfectly put together. Mussed and smudged with dirt as she was now, he probably thought she was horrified at the indignity.

Lord, she'd been such a bitch. And yet he'd been tender and patient throughout his courtship. He hadn't had a clue about the real her. She wasn't a goddess on a pedestal, although she'd pretended for years to please Daddy.

There'd been times when she'd pushed Jackson so hard, she'd flinched inside at the things she'd said, at the picture of the spoiled little rich girl she'd painted. And yet, not once had he shown a bit of disapproval. When she'd floated down the aisle on her father's arm, dressed in Vera Wang and looking like a princess, she'd panicked because the man standing beside the preacher didn't know her, and she didn't want him to feel cheated when he realized she wasn't the girl she'd portrayed.

But she knew him. She'd watched him for years. Spied on him when he didn't know it. She knew how he spoke with other men, not mincing words or holding back an epithet. She knew how he looked covered head to foot with dust and grime from riding herd on his family's ranch. She even knew what he looked like naked and aroused, because she'd followed him one day when he'd taken Carrie Molder to the river and made love to her on the grassy banks.

Every flex of sinewy muscle had enthralled her. And although she'd stayed a virgin, according to her father's wishes and despite the persistence of her many beaux, she'd known his large, rigid sex would fill her perfectly.

There'd never been any doubt in her mind that he was the one for her. But last Sunday, she'd realized she wasn't the woman to make him happy. Not if what he wanted was "Princess" Sammi Jo.

So she'd bolted, ignoring the shock in his eyes and the gasps and laughter chasing her out of the chapel.

But he'd been asking about the cabin, hadn't he? "It's dusty, but so am I."

His expression lost the sharp-edged anger that had accompanied his impromptu kidnapping. His jaw ground shut. A chilling bleakness crept across his handsome face.

She much preferred his anger. "Daddy's gonna have your balls for breakfast."

Heat flared in his hard gaze, again. And hadn't her mama said a man's anger could easily be turned into passion? She'd made promises, but so had he. She remembered every breathless moment she'd ever spent in his arms.

Adjusting her legs to the side, she watched him from under the fringe of her eyelashes, knowing the shift pushed her breasts against the thin tee she'd tucked into her sprayed-on designer jeans. She'd gone braless into Shooters, hoping for a chance to start over and show him the real her. The one who wanted him to see that she was a flesh-and-blood woman eager for his touch.

His gaze trailed down her chest, arrested on her spiking nipples, then slowly climbed again to lock with hers. Moisture seeped into her panties at the raw hunger reflected in his gaze.

"It's stuffy in here."

Without looking away, he reached beside him and shoved up the window to let in the hot breeze.

She bit her lip and feigned an embarrassed reluctance. "I'd be more comfortable if you'd unbuckle my belt. It's cuttin' into my waist, Jackson. I can hardly breathe."

His eyes narrowed, but he strode toward her, his fingers curling.

She straightened her legs and lay back as he reached for her buckle and flicked it open with practiced ease.

"Better?" he drawled.

"The button, too?" When it eased open, she let out a deep breath. "Better."

She knew what she looked like. Her long, blond hair spread over the plain comforter. He'd called it pretty as corn silk. Not the most poetic turn of phrase she'd ever been offered, but she'd melted knowing he thought it beautiful.

Melted like she did now, lying on a hard mattress with her pants undone and his large body blocking the light from the flickering flame.

"You have me all tied up, Jackson," she said, letting her drawl deepen into a sultry caress. "What do you intend to do with me now?"

His breath left him in a slow, even sigh. "I ought to pack you back into my truck and take you home."

"Whose home?"

His head canted. "What's your game now, Sammi Jo?"

"I don't know. You're the one who changed the rules," she said, raising her bound hand.

He blinked once then lowered his eyelids. "Maybe, for once, I wanted you to see me, Sammi Jo. The real me."

His statement so closely echoed her own thoughts, her breath paused. "The real you? I don't understand."

Jackson bent and skimmed his hands down the outsides of her thighs. Her breaths deepened. When he got to her knees, he tucked his hands between her legs and pushed them apart.

"Jackson?" His name came out in a breathless squeal.

He lowered his body until the hard ridge encased in his Wranglers snuggled against her crotch. One hand slipped beneath her, cupped her and held her close as he rocked between her legs. He braced himself on one elbow and bent his head to whisper in her ear. "Remember when I made you come like this, grindin' on your pussy?"

She whimpered, because then as now, the friction warmed her sex, split inside her pants.

"I wanted you so bad, I had to jack off before seeing you."

She shook her head. "You never talked like that before."

"I didn't want to shock you." His head lifted. His hard brown gaze bored into hers. "Tell me, baby, did you hold me off because you were worried I'd find out you aren't a virgin?"

His words chilled her instantly like a splash of icy water. She went still and fought the urge to scream, managing instead to give him her coldest stare. "I held you off because I wanted to see if you were man enough to take me."

His hips wedged between her thighs, and he pushed up on

both arms to stare down at her. "You shouldn't goad a man when he's hard as a post and not thinkin' with his brain."

"Never took you for a fucking genius, Jackson Lowry. Fact is, I was never after your brain."

"What was it you wanted?"

Anger rattled through her, shivering her breaths. "You. Like this. Making me do every nasty thing I'd ever dreamed of."

A hand slid beneath her head, fingers digging into her scalp. He gave her hair a hard tug. "I think you really do want that paddlin'. Don't you, baby?"

He'd called her sweetheart or honey before, but never baby, and he'd never looked at her before with passion glazing his eyes and firing his skin. His whole body hardened against hers as he let his full weight press her down into the mattress.

"I can't breathe."

"Good, then you can't argue with me."

She raised her eyebrows. "We gonna fight?"

"*I'm* gonna talk. *You'll* listen. Then I'll see about givin' you everything you deserve."

"Think you're the boss of me?"

"Yeah, I think it's what you've wanted all along." His expression sharpened, and he leaned toward her until his mouth touched hers.

His eyes were wide open, so even though hers were crossing, she kept them just as wide, glaring defiantly back.

His mouth suctioned her lips, then his teeth took a nip. She gasped and opened, and he swept inside, sliding his tongue along hers. He sucked again and drew her tongue into his mouth, pulling in a rhythm that mimicked the renewed surging of his hips.

Lord, she was close. Her eyelids drifted slowly downward.

Jackson broke the kiss; his body withdrew.

She tried to follow him, but the rope around her wrist was caught beneath her and kept her flat on the bed.

Jackson stood beside the bed and slowly stripped. "I'm bigger than you, stronger, and if I've treated you like porcelain it's because I didn't wanna hurt you."

She sniffed, pretending she wasn't growing more excited by everything he revealed. "I'm not fragile."

He shook his head. "No talkin'. Not unless I ask you a question."

"No talkin'? How long have you known me?"

Shirt and boots gone, Jackson unbuttoned his jeans and shoved them and his boxers to the floor. His gaze went to his erect cock, then lifted to meet hers again. "We've just been introduced. Decide if you want to know more now, or this stops."

"Again. Who made you the boss?"

One brow cocked. "It's my way—all the way."

Although she was secretly thrilled with his stern tone and even heavier-handed intentions, she wouldn't be who she was if she rolled over and gave a shy, "Yes, sir." And she only had one hand tied.

Still on her back, she scuffed off her boots and shoved off her pants, getting them as far as her knees and then wriggling like mad to pull her feet from the constricting denim.

Jackson stood beside the bed, his arms crossed over his chest. "Havin' problems there?"

"Don't you dare laugh."

His slow grin reflected pure male satisfaction.

She did the only thing she could, bunching up her feet and spreading her thighs.

His grin slipped, gaze arrowing toward her open sex.

Which made her feel awkward as hell. A flush burned her cheeks, but she didn't look away. Or flap her thighs closed, although the moment stretched, and she wondered if she should have been more ladylike.

"The shirt—lose it," Jackson growled without looking up.

She squirmed some more, but managed to push the tee up the rope and out of the way. With most of her body completely exposed, she began to worry.

He hadn't moved. His expression was unchanged, and so hard, she couldn't tell if he was disappointed. Sure, he'd felt her up plenty, under her clothes, in the dark, but he'd never seen her nude.

Maybe he thought her skin was too pasty. Maybe she should have completely shaved her bush rather than leaving a silky tuft on her mound. But she'd wanted him to decide how to trim it. Sammi Jo stretched down her free hand and covered herself.

Jackson untucked her legs and stripped off her jeans, then pulled her sideways until her legs fell over the mattress. When he knelt and pushed between her thighs, she didn't resist because his hands bracketed her pussy, both thumbs pulling apart her outer lips.

"I didn't lie," she said, her voice tiny.

"About which part?"

"Bein' a virgin."

"I wouldn't have cared. It's not something I expect."

"But you should know, right? Because I don't really know anything."

"You know plenty," he said, his eyes narrowing until she felt ready to purge herself of every guilty secret she'd ever kept.

"So, maybe I've touched a penis or two."

"Ever blown one?"

She shook her head. "Penises are kinda ugly. At least, I used to think that," she said glancing down at Jackson's fine straight cock.

"You'll get used to it."

Did he mean he'd want her after this weekend? "Maybe it's an acquired taste. Like snails."

His nose wrinkled up in disgust. "It won't taste like snails."

"Didn't think it would." She chewed her lips to keep from grinning. Then she had another thought. "Maybe you won't like the way I taste."

"You asking me to eat you out?"

Her breath left in a whoosh. "Do you always talk like this to women?"

"I try to be a gentleman."

"You just can't manage it with me?"

"You wanted it real. This is as real as it gets with me, Sammi Jo." He looked down, drawing her glance right along as he fisted his cock. "My dick's so hard all I can really think about is shovin' deep inside your pussy. Or your ass."

"My ass?" she gasped, appalled.

"Yeah, we'll get to that. Don't jump ahead."

"Tonight?"

"Hell no. Have to save somethin' for the weddin' night."

Her heart stuttered, then sped up again, pounding furiously inside her chest. "Weddin' night?"

"Didn't I mention it before? I called the reverend. He'll speak our vows come Monday morning."

"You still wanna marry me?"

"Let's get this straight. I will always wanna marry you— whether you chicken out again Monday or thirty years from now."

"But you don't really know me. Maybe I did you a favor."

"You think so?" His lids drooped as he scanned her pussy and breasts before landing on her flushed face. "Think I don't know there's a woman who wants me to paddle her ass and fuck her 'til she's blind? I *know* it, baby. You flash me those pretty blue eyes with a hint of sparkle just before you send me runnin' to get you a glass of ice tea. I know you. You want me to turn you over my knee. Put my foot down."

She breathed in sharply, secretly pleased by his firm tone. "Oh, do I? Maybe I really do get powerful thirsts."

His finger skimmed between her lips and came up glistening. He poked it in his mouth and sucked it. "I like the way you taste."

She reached behind her, grabbed the pillow, and tossed it at his head.

Jackson laughed, then buried his face between her legs, eliciting a squeal.

At the first tug of his lips against her clitoris, her back arched. "Jackson!" After that, she didn't have the breath to scream or even whisper. Whimpering, a little moaning—she knew she sounded like she was dying, but didn't care. His tongue flicked the hard knot, then swirled in slow circles, causing her vagina to constrict and relax convulsively as she came.

She hadn't the energy, the breath, to beg him to end it, and instead held her own breasts, squeezing them to comfort herself as her head turned side to side. Her whole body trembled, shivers shaking the thighs clasping his face.

When he lifted his head, revealing blurred lips and wet, reddened cheeks, she didn't resist as he pressed her thighs to fall apart again. A finger traced her slit, then tucked inside it to swirl in the fluids he'd coaxed from her body. It drove deeper and deeper, then pulled free. "No hymen," he whispered, then gave a waggle of his eyebrows.

"I didn't lie."

"I know that. I don't want to hurt you. It's better this way."

"Better? God, you're gonna kill me."

He chuckled and pushed her to the center of the mattress. When he came down on his elbows, his hips wedged between her thighs, his cock aligned with her folds, Sammi Jo felt something loosen inside her. "I'm sorry."

"Stop," he said with sharp shake of his head. "I'm sorry too. Don't be scared anymore, Sammi Jo. I know exactly what I'm gettin'. I won't ever want to toss you back."

"I love you."

"I know."

Her lips pouted. "You aren't gonna say it back?"

"I've said it 'til I'm blue in the face."

So Jackson wasn't a romantic, she could live with that. "That's not the part you said was blue."

"Let me show you what you mean to me." He pushed up on his arms. "Go ahead and put him right at your—"

"Hole?"

His nose wrinkled, and he shook his head. "You like that better than pussy?"

She wrinkled her nose right back. "Not really. Maybe we should name it."

His lips twitched. "Like you would a dog or a puss—?"

"Stop!" She giggled, then lifted her head and kissed him. Her free hand closed around his thick, hot shaft, and she placed it at her entrance. She moved it around and wet it, listening to the lewd, moist sounds that reminded her of their hot kisses, and then she tilted her hips a fraction to capture the blunt, round head. Lord, it felt huge as he held still, poised to stroke inward. "I know it's supposed to fit…"

His expression softened. "Tell me something."

"Now?"

"What did your daddy say to you when he was walkin' you down the aisle."

"Again: *now?*" she whined and wriggled, trying to draw him into her body.

"I gotta know what had you runnin' out o' the church."

She sighed. "He stepped on my dress."

"You were upset about a little footprint?"

"No. Just before we left the vestibule, I told him I couldn't go through with it. That you didn't have a clue what kind of person I was. I tried to draw back, but he stepped on my dress."

"Your daddy was tryin' to talk you into marryin' me? I thought he didn't like me much."

She snorted. "He likes you plenty. But he thought you deserved a little hazin' so you'd have to work harder to earn my hand. Said Mama's daddy put him through the wringer—he was just payin' it forward."

His mouth stretched into a wide grin. "You know I'm gonna have to paddle your ass. Your daddy's been on everyone's shit list."

"Daddy's a big boy. He'll get over the embarrassment." *Speaking of big boys...* "You're right there. How much more encouragement do you need?"

Jackson pushed, giving a little circular motion that eased the tip of him into her body.

"That screwin'?"

He laughed. "Don't, not now. I wanna go slow."

"What about what I want?" she said, knowing she sounded like a child denied candy, but she was greedy for it.

"What do you want, baby?"

"You so deep inside me we're like one person."

"Gettin' there. Swear." The next stroke was deeper, and his girth caused a pinching pain inside her.

She must have winced, because he stopped moving. Sweat beaded on his forehead; his lips were drawn into a thin, firm line—as though he was in pain.

"That didn't hurt much. Don't stop on my account."

"You sure?"

No, but it would be the shortest denouement in the history of sex if he didn't hurry it up. "Yes."

He moved again, a tentative glide that pushed him deeper still. Her inner muscles clamped around him, squeezing. "Sorry."

"No, feels great," he rasped.

She arched a brow. "Any time now, Jackson. I know there's more to this."

A bark of laughter erupted, and he came down on top of her, hugged her close, then rolled.

Sitting nailed to his lap, she blinked as she tried to steady her breaths. "I like this view." She wasn't lying. Looking down at her herself, at her flushed skin, tight nipples and quivering belly, gave her an inkling of what was going on behind those dark eyes of his. His broad chest was sturdy, thickly muscled, hairy—so masculine and yummy she wanted to lick him like a doe would a salt block. And lord, his stomach was tight, the musculature so well-defined she could sink fingers in the deep grooves.

The most interesting sight, however, was where their bodies joined. She wasn't quite flush with his pubic bone. His shaft disappeared inside her. She had the urge to watch as she rose and fell to see what it looked like, and began to move, bracing her hands on his chest but curving her neck to watch. He was slick from her juices, reddened—ridged with heavy veins she could feel as she pushed down, up, then down again.

His hands clutched her hips and tightened, but she shook her head. "I wanna see."

"Then watch this," he whispered. A hand pressed against her lower tummy, his thumb rubbed on her clit, then lifted the thin hood covering it. It was red, bulbous and glistening.

The cooler air felt like a caress, and she gave a little moan.

Jackson raised his other hand and licked two fingertips, then touched her clit. It was a gentle caress, but the callus on his fingertip scraped, and she let out a shaky gasp.

"Too much?"

With her breaths shortening and her whole body trembling, she placed a hand over his and pressed his fingers harder against the nub. Then she renewed her movements, climbing up his shaft, then shoving downward, swirling when she hit the base, then rising again to repeat the process.

Her eyelids drifted downward and she concentrated on every sensation: the girth stretching her channel, the hot moisture lubricating her walls, the chafe of his pubic hair, and the tantalizing rub of his fingertips. She moved faster, breasts bouncing, her moans chopped apart as she landed harder and harder against him.

When her orgasm hit, it was better than anything her own hand had ever delivered. She ground to a halt, hot and cold waves washing over her shivering skin. Pleasure exploded, blinding her. "*Ohgodohgod!*"

Swaying, she welcomed the strength in the hands soothing her breasts, her belly. When it passed, she opened her eyes.

Jackson's gaze locked with hers. His features were tight, his eyes glittered with moisture. "Baby, that was beautiful."

She gave him a tired smile then slowly melted toward his chest. His arms enclosed her, hugging her tightly. A kiss landed on her temple. "Rest a while."

"But...you?"

"I've waited this long. Another little while won't kill me."

Sammi Jo nuzzled into the corner of his neck. "I'm glad I waited."

Jackson rubbed her bottom as she nestled closer. A gust of

hot breath ruffled the hair stuck to her cheek. "Don't think I've forgotten."

Her bottom pushed up against his hand. "What's it gonna be?" she said with a lazy drawl. "A lick for every hour I made you wait?"

He tapped her butt, then rubbed the spot hard. "Let's make it two."

SHE DON'T STAY THE NIGHT

Anna Meadows

S he should have known the first time she saw him, but he was
too quiet and still. More than that, he was respectful. Boys
with that kind of wildness usually ran their mouths. But if she
had seen the set to the muscles around his eyes, she might have
caught the first hint of the recklessness that would make him
ride off on *los pasos de la muerte* years later. He did not have
the look of a boy who would laugh at death, but one who might
look it in the eye, waiting for it to flinch.

Adabella was fifteen the day Buckley Carver wandered onto
her family's land. He was the same age, *mas o menos*. She
couldn't know for sure. He never would tell anyone his birthday.
He didn't want Adabella's mother stringing *la piñata estrella* up
the ash tree, and he sure as hell didn't want the men singing
"*Las Mañanitas*," so off-key the cows would groan.

He'd been small and dirty that first day, too proud to look
hungry. Adabella had brought him inside like a stray cat. Her
mother said it was because that was the first time Adabella

had seen a blond boy, a real one. Everyone in the Rocíos' piece of the *llano* was dark-haired, except for the few women who combed peroxide through their coarse hair each Sunday. *Las rubias de bote*, her mother called them, bottle blondes. But Buckley Carver had come that way, and to Adabella it was as strange as the pink horses her cousins swore roamed some far corner of the plain, although they knew of no one who had seen one himself.

Adabella made the boy *higaditos de fandango* with the eggs from her mother's chickens. Some were blue-shelled, others green; Adabella's cousins would eat neither. She warmed tortillas left from breakfast while the boy found a screwdriver in a kitchen drawer and reattached a brass knob that had come loose from a cabinet, like he lived there and it was his job to see to the repairs.

"What are you doing?" Adabella asked him.

"It needs fixing," he said. "I know how to fix it."

She didn't stop him. She kept her eye on the stove. It was the first time she'd turned tortillas on the open flame with her fingers instead of warming them on the *comal*.

Her mother didn't startle when she saw Buckley Carver at the kitchen table. She only nodded at him once, like she'd been expecting him.

"And what can you do, *chico blanco*?" her mother asked him.

"Anything anybody can teach me," he said.

Her mother gave another nod, curt this time, one of respect. She didn't want much out of men but that they were willing to work. She didn't ask where he'd run from, or how he'd come by the halo of blue around his right eye, like the nebulae Adabella's father found through the telescope. When Adabella lifted her hand to point at the bruise, her mother slapped her fingers like they were moths flitting around a skein of *huacaya* wool.

Her mother took to him because he cleaned up nice, her cousins because they could teach him to say *pendejo* and *gabacho*. They called him *el caballo blanco*, the white horse, from one of the *corridos* they sang as they passed around the *mescal* on Sunday nights. Buckley Carver would come to a happier end than the horse in the song, they said, but he would die on the *llano*, like they would, like *el caballo* had, because they could see he was already falling in love with how the raw turquoise of the sky met the gold of the earth.

They liked him too because he never passed them. However long he'd been hungry must've killed a growth spurt, because he never got taller than the men in Adabella's family. They liked him better for that, because the only thing worse than a *gringo* was one who had to look down at everybody else. But he looked taller for how straight he stood, like he was staring the whole desert right in the eye, no matter how that unburnished gold seemed to spread to the far hems of the world, no matter how big the clouds that unfurled in the blue.

Adabella did not worry about her mother turning the boy out, because her mother knew that Buckley Carver would not survive on another *hacienda*. Not because he was too soft for the work—even at fifteen, calluses had already made his hands rough as a cat's tongue—but because he was a gentle soul, *un tierno*. Watching how roughly the men of other families handled *los broncos* and the cattle would have broken him, as though he were one of those wild horses.

But the Rocío men were not that way. Their Aztec blood made them want to do things quickly. It was not that they treated the bulls with soft hands, but that they offered them the respect they would show a rival. They looked *los toros* in their eyes, assuring them that they would win, but that they also understood the fight to come. For over fifty years, they had branded not with hot iron but with *hielo seco*, dry ice brought by a man in a green truck. The children watched for the green truck because they could snatch little pieces off their fathers' blocks. The boys dared each other to hold them in their palms, and the girls liked watching cats chase the bits as they skittered across the floor.

Adabella had watched Buckley the first time the men showed him how to cold-brand cattle. He froze the brand on the dry ice, wisps of vapor rising off the block like mist from a pond, and he pressed the chilled copper against a shaved patch on the animal's thigh. The cow didn't like it, but neither did it cry out like it would have at the heat. Instead it huffed as though stung by a horsefly. The cow sulked away, and Adabella's cousins slapped Buckley on the back and told him he was a good *vaquerito*.

Within a couple of weeks, the cow's coat had grown back, and the outline of the Rocío brand showed in pale hair. "It kills the hair cells that make the color," Adabella's father had told Buckley when he came to inspect the boy's work. "The color doesn't come, so the hair grows back white." He patted the cow above its brand, and the animal grazed out into the sun. "We'll make a *vaquero* of you yet," he said. "You may be *pálido, como los conquistadores*, but you are more like the *vaqueros* of the mission, I think."

Adabella wanted to tell Buckley that it was her father's highest compliment, especially to a *gringo*, but that would have meant stepping out from behind the ash tree and admitting she had been listening.

"Everything the northern cowboys are, it came from us," her father told Buckley. "When *los españoles* could not keep track of their own cows, they used us."

Wind threaded through the ash tree's leaves, shifting the light, and Adabella noticed that *el caballo blanco* was barefoot.

It surprised her every time she saw his toes, brown with dust, at the hem of his jeans, even though he was that way half the year. That was something else that earned her father's admiration, because it was how *vaqueros* worked the land hundreds of years ago. No one would have blamed Buckley for wearing shoes year-round—half of Adabella's cousins did—but the one time she asked him, Buckley said he liked having nothing between him and the ground. By now the soles of his feet had learned to take the heat and coarse earth, so he only wore boots from late fall, when the trees held only a few fire-colored leaves, to the first week the desert amethysts burst into bloom in the spring. Sometimes, he'd even go barefoot far enough into fall that he'd be surprised to feel the crunch of iced-over leaves under his feet, and Adabella's mother would yell out the window, "*¡Dios mío!*" and tell him to get his boots on.

Buckley watched the cow, its body turning to show the pale shape of the family brand. "What do you do about a white horse?" he asked Adabella's father.

"You'd have to hold the brand on a little longer, and it'd kill the hair cells, *también*, so the brand would stay clear," her father said. "But it doesn't matter. No white horses 'round here."

Adabella caught Buckley's wince. She wanted to tell him it didn't mean anything. Her father didn't know the nickname her cousins had tied to Buckley Carver within his first month on the *cortijo*. But the shadows between the barn and the ash tree were her hiding place, and even when her father left to check on the half-acre of blue corn, she did not slip out into the light. It was where she watched *el caballo blanco* in the wintertime as he wrapped the red *faja* around his waist and tied it in place. She stayed quiet as he pulled on his jean jacket or, in colder weather, a heavier *chaqueta*, and set his *espuelas*, the stars of metal on his heels glinting like ice in the riverbed. In summer, she made out the muscles in his back through his shirt and the shadow of his hair as it fell in his face. She always wondered how he kept his fingernails clean even when the dirt weighed down the hems of his jeans.

She was almost eighteen when her mother told her she was to go and live with her aunt up north at the end of the summer. That was about the time Buckley tried his first *paso de la muerte*, a death ride on a wild horse, bareback. Only a handful of the men on the *cortijo* were crazy enough to try it, and more than a few of them had needed a bone or two set after.

Adabella's mother had seen that wildness in Buckley's eyes before anyone else had. She saw him thinking of the stories of *los pasos de la muerte*. "Don't do it," she said. "You're a fine *vaquero* as you are. You don't need a broken arm to prove it."

But *el caballo blanco* took his favorite mount from the *remuda* and rode out onto the *llano* until he got close enough to a *mesteño*, a wild mare, to throw himself on its back. His favorite horse grazed its way back to the stable, and he rode out toward where the blue met the ground, his thighs gripping the back of a creature as wild and sleepless as he was.

A man could die that way. Men had. If he misjudged on the moving mount, or the tame horse startled, he could be trampled. If he got on, the *mesteño* could still buck and throw him. It was for that reason Adabella did not say goodbye to *el caballo blanco*. She did not want to see him wrapping the *faja* around his waist and think it might be the last time.

El caballo blanco did not write to her, and she did not write to him, although her aunt made her pen letters at least twice a week. "The girls your age, they all use the telephone now," her aunt said as she watched over the desk where her niece wrote, tapping a pencil on any words Adabella had not written neatly enough.

So Adabella wrote to her mother, asking about the chickens with the blue eggs, to her father, wondering had he seen *los meteoritos* through the brass telescope. She wrote to her cousins, asking after the man in the green truck who delivered *el hielo seco*, or telling their wives how happy she was for the latest picture of their children. But she did not write to the silence that was *el caballo blanco*, and she did not ask about him or his *pasos de la muerte*.

Her aunt taught her to grow out her nails; bitter melon oil on the tips kept her from biting. She taught her not to click her teeth like her cousins did, to set her shoulders straight instead of slouching like a little girl, to wear *un brasier* under her blouses. She taught her to chop onions so finely that Adabella wanted to fling them into the night sky to see if the pieces would stick in the dark in the shape of constellations.

At night, Adabella imagined *el caballo*, his callus-thickened fingers fastening the bright *faja*. The wind would brush his hair off his face like wheat stalks, and his hands would be on the back of some wild horse who might not buck him off because it recognized they were similar creatures.

She thought of his hands on a mare's mane, and felt a jealousy like the sting of dry ice spread inside her ribcage and then down through her body. She thought of the tension in his thighs as he fought to stay on the *mesteño*, his feet bare-sand rough in the summer, winking with the silver of spurs in the winter.

Some nights, if she was not careful, she thought of him hardening against the button-fly of his jeans. She thought of her thighs gripping his body as tightly as his held onto the backs of wild horses. She imagined unfastening each of those buttons, so slow he groaned with waiting, while he cupped her breasts through the shell-colored lace of the lingerie she now wore even to bed. Those were nights she did not sleep, and in the morning her aunt told her not to read so much at night, not even *la Biblia*, because all those words wouldn't let her rest.

Adabella came back taller, though still not tall; she was the first woman in three generations to break five feet, and her aunt swore it was good posture and the corn silk tea she made the girl drink three times a day. Adabella could now turn tortillas on the stove without shifting her weight from one bare foot to another or humming her cousins' *corridos*. She had learned patience, and could listen without fidgeting to the men who visited her father, because her aunt's church had a priest who repeated himself so often the homilies lasted twice as long.

Her mother clasped her hands and took a look at the girl who might now pass for a woman. "Yes," her mother said. "Good." She was happiest to see that Adabella's hair now gleamed down her back; she had learned to comb it each night and each morning, so it was never the full cloud of tangles it had been when she left.

Adabella did not ask about *el caballo blanco* or if *los pasos de la muerte* had killed him. She did not see him until a little before dawn, when she woke to a horse's soft whinny just outside her window. At first, she thought its color was a trick of the light, that the pale coat was catching the glow off a strawberry moon. But when she ran out into the night air she saw it was true; its coat was a blend of soft brown, white, and auburn that looked rose-colored from a distance.

The horse wandered out of range of the house's light. She ran after it, the wind billowing her nightgown behind her. The grass was cool under her bare feet, and it let off its green scent so the whole world smelled like lemons by the time the horse stopped near the ash tree.

Buckley Carver came out from the tree's shadow. He was a little taller, the muscles of his thighs a little more visible inside his jeans, even in the dark. His hair had grown out long enough he had to toss his head like a colt to get it off his face. His forearms were sun-darkened enough that they did not shine under the moon.

He stroked the horse's side. "Pretty, isn't she?"

"It's real?" Adabella asked. The mare had no brand or harness, and she had heard of pink horses only in her family's stories.

"I'm surprised as anybody," he said. "She's a strawberry roan. *La ruana*. Lightest one I ever heard of."

His Spanish had always made her crazy. It was awful, even for as many words as he knew, but hearing it in his northerner's accent drew wetness from her until she could feel it on the lace between her thighs. "You didn't write to me."

"Your mother sent you away to become a lady," he said. "Not to become a lady for me."

It had never been about that. Adabella's mother was unconcerned with her finding a husband; she would soon enough, her mother thought, and if she didn't, there was no harm in her staying to help care for the *cortijo*.

Adabella's mother had sent her to her aunt because she was learning her manners from the men on the land. No daughter of Teresa Rocío would run through the apple trees with her hair uncombed and her breasts free beneath her nightgown.

Adabella raked a few cautious fingers over *la ruana*'s coat. "Do my cousins know about her?"

"You kidding? She scares easy. I'm not getting her around them." He offered Adabella his hand. "You want to take her out?"

"You've ridden her?"

"I don't ride her," he said. "I'm too big for her." He patted the horse where there was no saddle. "She'll like you though.

You're both little."

"I'm not getting on her. She's wild."

"She knows me," Buckley said. "And I told her about you."

The horse didn't startle at Buckley's touch. "How do you get her to stay?"

"She don't stay the night, but if you let her go, she'll let you find her the next day."

"I don't know how to ride bareback."

"I'll teach you. Her withers are just about flat. She'll never fit a saddle, but she'll be good for you to learn on. I'll get you on her tomorrow." He saw the first blush of the sun on the horizon, and sent *la ruana* off toward the thread of light. "She don't like being around in the morning." *La ruana* grew smaller in the distance, a flush of pink in the moonlight.

El caballo blanco nodded goodnight, but Adabella grabbed him before he could go. She slid one hand on the back of his neck, the other on his waist, and although he startled, he didn't pull away.

She kissed him like she had thought of kissing him at night, his tongue hot between her lips. She still hated him for his silence, but she could not help thinking of him on his nightly *paso de la muerte*, chasing a pink horse that may or not have been a trick of the light. She thought of *la ruana* trusting him both for his sureness and his humility, his rough fingertips but gentle hands.

She gripped his thighs through his jeans, her body close enough to feel him harden. She ran her hands over his shirt, the fabric sticking to the perspiration on his chest. It was another thing to hate him for—that he was dressed, while she was in her nightgown with her hair unbrushed. She let him feel it when she untied the *faja*, lifted his shirt, and dug her nails into his lower back until she could smell the salt and iron of his blood. She heard the catch in his breathing, but it only got him harder.

He ran his hands through her hair, his fingers catching on new tangles. He grabbed her so hard she felt as though his hands would burn through her nightgown, leaving her naked. It made her wonder how she had gone years looking at him without knowing what his hands felt like. The only touch of his she'd ever known was the passing brush of his forearm or him helping her onto a horse. She wanted every touch she hadn't had, like she'd shared a deep sleep with the girls in the *cuentos de hadas*, the fairytales of her aunt's storybooks.

She pushed him up against the ash tree and slipped loose each of the buttons on his fly—not slowly like she had imagined, but quickly enough that he seemed surprised to have that part of him hard and naked so fast. She knew from the set of his teeth that she'd ignited the same wildness that sent him off on *los pasos de la muerte*.

He grabbed the backs of her thighs, taking her weight as she gripped her legs around his waist. It was dark enough, and she was drunk enough on the heat of his body that she might not have known he'd turned her if she hadn't felt the ridges of the ash tree's bark digging into her back. He pushed up her nightgown and pulled aside the lace between her thighs, her wetness coming off on his fingers.

At first she wished he couldn't feel it, but she heard his groan, like he wanted it. His fingers swam over her as though he'd found the sugar water at the heart of an agave.

She reached between their bodies and stroked her fingertips over him, provoking him until he let her guide him inside her. It hurt like she wanted it to, like tapping her fingers on dry ice, like her nails on his back must have hurt him. She thought she felt him get harder. He heard the soft noise from the back of her throat and asked her whether he should stop, but the sound and warmth of his voice on her neck made her open. She bit his shoulder to show him how it hurt, like dry ice, so cold it stung with heat.

He bent his head to catch her mouth, and she drew in his tongue. His hands fidgeted with her hair and her nightgown, wanting to touch that agave heart again, but he didn't, and she knew he was thinking of the calluses on the tips of his fingers.

She grabbed his hand and forced it between them, guiding his fingers to *la perla*, water-slicked as the moon in the river. Those calluses gave his touch the warmth and grain of late afternoon sand, like it was the desert making love to her, the whole sky, all that blue.

It was winter the day she became the wife of *el caballo blanco*. Adabella's mother strung a dozen *piñatas estrellas*, each as blue as the *llano* sky, from the ash tree to mark the day. The children were already sleeping off the sugar from the wedding *cajeta*, and did not care for knocking them down. It was cold enough the paper gathered hoarfrost, and it glittered in the December morning like amethyst, blue and raw.

By Christmas, the ice would thicken and curl into petals and frost flowers, and Adabella and Buckley would see it from their window, *una estrella fugaz* held in the ash branches. In the spring the ice would give, and the paper would yield its thorn apples and coins of sugar cane like constellations letting stardust fall to Earth.

La ruana came to the ash tree just after midnight. The Rocío men did not see her come; they thought *el caballo blanco* and his wife were lying together for the first time. Buckley helped Adabella onto the horse's blush-colored back, and then vanished into the dark. The mare's body was warm under her thighs and hands, her mane full of the scent of sweat and earth and dust-covered strawberry blossoms.

La ruana knew the way to the wild corner of the *llano*. Adabella found Buckley out there, beneath those handfuls of stars, on the back of a horse too pale to be branded. They rode *la ruana* and that white *mesteño* toward the edge of the sky, until the sunrise turned the horizon pink as rock salt, and it was time to let them go.

ABOUT THE AUTHORS

RANDI ALEXANDER writes erotic romance and has published with The Wild Rose Press. When she's not writing about cowboys, she's biking, snorkeling, or practicing her drumming in hopes of someday forming a tropical-rock band.

CHEYENNE BLUE, who also writes as Maggie Kinsella and Charles LeDuc, has appeared in over sixty anthologies, including *Best Women's Erotica*, *Best Lesbian Erotica*, *Best Lesbian Love Stories*, *Girl Crazy*, *Lesbian Cowboys*, *Girl Crush*, and *Mammoth Best New Erotica*. She will have several stories featured in upcoming anthologies in 2011 and 2012.

MICHAEL BRACKEN, an award-winning writer of fiction, non-fiction, and advertising copy, is the author of almost nine hundred short stories, several of which have appeared in Cleis Press anthologies.

CHAPARRITA has a fiery passion for sex, writing, travel, yoga, and anything juicy and stimulating. She'll be featured in *Best Women's Erotica 2012* and has been featured in *Clean Sheets*. She's lived and loved around the world, but currently calls the U.S. her home.

NENA CLEMENTS lives with her husband and the last two of her four children and a whole mess of animals on a quiet little place she refers to as "her piece of heaven" in rural Arkansas. She loves to transport her readers to a place where "happy ever after" is a reality.

SEDONA FOX is new to the romance and erotica world. She resides in Pennsylvania with her loving husband and animals. Currently, Sedona is working on a series of paranormal romance novels.

TAHIRA IQBAL is a UK-based writer who currently works in the film and TV industry, but writing is and will always be her first love. You can find her erotic vampire short story "The Queen," in the *Red Velvet and Absinthe* anthology published by Cleis Press.

LORELEI JAMES, *New York Times* and *USA Today Best-selling* author, pens the Rough Riders and Blacktop Cowboys series—contemporary erotic western romances about cowboys and the women who love them. Lorelei's books have won the Romantic Times Reviewer's Choice Award and the CAPA Award. Lorelei lives in western South Dakota.

CAT JOHNSON is known for her creative research and marketing techniques. Consequently, some of her closest friends/

book consultants wear combat or cowboy boots for a living. She owns a collection of camouflage and western footwear for book signings, and she sponsors real live bull riders.

M. MARIE lives in the heart of downtown Toronto, Canada, and has a profound passion for art and the theatre. Having previously won several young writer awards for her poetry and short stories, she is excited to now be enchanting new readers with her erotic writing.

LISSA MATTHEWS lives in North Carolina, right smack dab in the middle of NASCAR country, with her husband, two children, and seven cats. When not at the races, she can be found drinking coffee, writing, baking, or watching college football. Sometimes she can be found doing all these at the same time...

ANNA MEADOWS is a part-time executive assistant, part-time Sapphic housewife. Her work appears in six Cleis Press anthologies, including *Girls Who Bite*. She lives and writes in Northern California.

CARI QUINN, by day, saves the world one Photoshop file at a time in her job as a graphic designer. At night, she writes erotic romance, drinks way too much coffee, and plays her music way too loud. Oh, and she laughs. A lot.

CHARLENE TEGLIA has garnered several honors for her novels, including the prestigious *Romantic Times* Reviewer's Choice Award. Her work has been translated into Spanish, Thai, and German, excerpted in *Complete Woman*, and selected by the Rhapsody, Doubleday, and Literary Guild Book Clubs.

KIMBER VALE is an avid reader, writer, and gardener. She worked as an RN in a previous life. Currently, she raises three small people and puts fantasies to computer screen.

ABOUT
THE EDITOR

DELILAH DEVLIN is a prolific and award-winning author of erotica and erotic romance with a rapidly expanding reputation for writing deliciously edgy stories with complex characters. Whether creating dark, erotically-charged paranormal worlds or richly descriptive historical and contemporary stories that ring with authenticity, Delilah Devlin "pens in uncharted territory that will leave the readers breathless and hungering for more" (*Paranormal Reviews*). Ms. Devlin has published more than a hundred erotic stories of multiple genres and lengths. She is published by Avon, Berkley, Kensington, Atria/Strebor, Black Lace, Harlequin Spice, Ellora's Cave, Samhain Publishing, and Cleis Press. Her published print titles include *Into the Darkness, Seduced by Darkness, Darkness Burning, Darkness Captured, Down in Texas, Texas Men, Ravished by a Viking,* and *Enslaved by a Viking.* She has appeared in Cleis Press's *Lesbian Cowboys, Girl Crush, Fairy Tale Lust, Lesbian Lust, Passion, Lesbian Cops, Dream Lover, Carnal Machines,* and *Best Erotic Romance (2012). Girls Who Bite,* Delilah's first effort as an editor for a Cleis collection, was released in 2011.

Bestselling Erotica for Couples

Sweet Life
Erotic Fantasies for Couples
Edited by Violet Blue

Your ticket to a front row seat for first-time spankings, breathtaking role-playing scenes, sex parties, women who strap it on and men who love to take it, not to mention threesomes of every combination.
ISBN 978-1-57344-133-9 $14.95

Sweet Life 2
Erotic Fantasies for Couples
Edited by Violet Blue

"This is a we-did-it-you-can-too anthology of real couples playing out their fantasies." —Lou Paget, author of *365 Days of Sensational Sex*
ISBN 978-1-57344-167-4 $15.95

Sweet Love
Erotic Fantasies for Couples
Edited by Violet Blue

"If you ever get a chance to try out your number-one fantasies in real life—and I assure you, there will be more than one—say yes. It's well worth it. May this book, its adventurous authors, and the daring and satisfied characters be your guiding inspiration."—Violet Blue
ISBN 978-1-57344-381-4 $14.95

Afternoon Delight
Erotica for Couples
Edited by Alison Tyler

"Alison Tyler evokes a world of heady sensuality where fantasies are fearlessly explored and dreams gloriously realized."
—Barbara Pizio, Executive Editor, *Penthouse Variations*
ISBN 978-1-57344-341-8 $14.95

Three-Way
Erotic Stories
Edited by Alison Tyler

"Three means more of everything. Maybe I'm greedy, but when it comes to sex, I like more. More fingers. More tongues. More limbs. More tangling and wrestling on the mattress."
ISBN 978-1-57344-193-3 $15.95

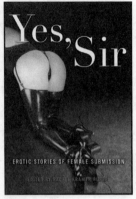

Red Hot Erotic Romance

Obsessed
Erotic Romance for Women
Edited by Rachel Kramer Bussel

These stories sizzle with the kind of obsession that is fueled by our deepest desires, the ones that hold couples together, the ones that haunt us and don't let go. Whether just-blooming passions, rekindled sparks or reinvented relationships, these lovers put the object of their obsession first.
ISBN 978-1-57344-718-8 $14.95

Passion
Erotic Romance for Women
Edited by Rachel Kramer Bussel

Love and sex have always been intimately intertwined—and *Passion* shows just how delicious the possibilities are when they mingle in this sensual collection edited by award-winning author Rachel Kramer Bussel.
ISBN 978-1-57344-415-6 $14.95

Girls Who Bite
Lesbian Vampire Erotica
Edited by Delilah Devlin

Bestselling romance writer Delilah Devlin and her contributors add fresh girl-on-girl blood to the pantheon of the paranormal. The stories in *Girls Who Bite* are varied, un-expected, and soul-scorching.
ISBN 978-1-57344-715-7 $14.95

Irresistible
Erotic Romance for Couples
Edited by Rachel Kramer Bussel

This prolific editor has gathered the most popular fantasies and created a sizzling, no-holds-barred collection of explicit encounters in which couples turn their deepest desires into reality.
978-1-57344-762-1 $14.95

Heat Wave
Hot, Hot, Hot Erotica
Edited by Alison Tyler

What could be sexier or more seductive than bare, sun-warmed skin? Bestselling erotica author Alison Tyler gathers explicit stories of summer sex bursting with the sweet eroticism of swimsuits, sprinklers, and ripe strawberries.
ISBN 978-1-57344-710-2 $15.95

Best Erotica Series

"Gets racier every year."—*San Francisco Bay Guardian*

**Buy 4 books,
Get 1 *FREE****

Best Women's Erotica 2012
Edited by Violet Blue
ISBN 978-1-57344-755-3 $15.95

Best Women's Erotica 2011
Edited by Violet Blue
ISBN 978-1-57344-423-1 $15.95

Best Women's Erotica 2010
Edited by Violet Blue
ISBN 978-1-57344-373-9 $15.95

Best Bondage Erotica 2012
Edited by Rachel Kramer Bussel
ISBN 978-1-57344-754-6 $15.95

Best Bondage Erotica 2011
Edited by Rachel Kramer Bussel
ISBN 978-1-57344-426-2 $15.95

Best Fetish Erotica
Edited by Cara Bruce
ISBN 978-1-57344-355-5 $15.95

Best Lesbian Erotica 2012
Edited by Kathleen Warnock. Selected and
introduced by Sinclair Sexsmith.
ISBN 978-1-57344-752-2 $15.95

Best Lesbian Erotica 2011
Edited by Kathleen Warnock.
Selected and introduced by Lea DeLaria.
ISBN 978-1-57344-425-5 $15.95

Best Lesbian Erotica 2010
Edited by Kathleen Warnock.
Selected and introduced by BETTY.
ISBN 978-1-57344-375-3 $15.95

Best Gay Erotica 2012
Edited by Richard Labonté. Selected and
introduced by Larry Duplechan.
ISBN 978-1-57344-753-9, $15.95

Best Gay Erotica 2011
Edited by Richard Labonté.
Selected and introduced by Kevin Killian.
ISBN 978-1-57344-424-8 $15.95

Best Gay Erotica 2010
Edited by Richard Labonté. Selected and
introduced by Blair Mastbaum.
ISBN 978-1-57344-374-6 $15.95

In Sleeping Beauty's Bed
Erotic Fairy Tales
By Mitzi Szereto
ISBN 978-1-57344-367-8 $16.95

Can't Help the Way That I Feel
Sultry Stories of African American Love
Edited by Lori Bryant-Woolridge
ISBN 978-1-57344-386-9 $14.95

Making the Hook-Up
Edgy Sex with Soul
Edited by Cole Riley
ISBN 978-1-57344-3838 $14.95

*** Free book of equal or lesser value. Shipping and applicable sales tax extra.
Cleis Press • (800) 780-2279 • orders@cleispress.com
www.cleispress.com**

Fuel Your Fantasies

Carnal Machines
Steampunk Erotica
Edited by D. L. King

In this decadent fusing of technology and romance, outstanding contemporary erotica writers use the enthralling possibilities of the 19th-century steam age to tease and titillate.
ISBN 978-1-57344-654-9 $14.95

The Sweetest Kiss
Ravishing Vampire Erotica
Edited by D.L. King

These sanguine tales give new meaning to the term "dead sexy" and feature beautiful bloodsuckers whose desires go far beyond blood.
ISBN 978-1-57344-371-5 $15.95

The Handsome Prince
Gay Erotic Romance
Edited by Neil Plakcy

A bawdy collection of bedtime stories brimming with classic fairy tale characters, reimagined and recast for any man who has dreamt of the day his prince will come. These sexy stories fuel fantasies and remind us all of the power of true romance.
ISBN 978-1-57344-659-4 $14.95

Daughters of Darkness
Lesbian Vampire Tales
Edited by Pam Keesey

"A tribute to the sexually aggressive woman and her archetypal roles, from nurturing goddess to dangerous predator."—*The Advocate*
ISBN 978-1-57344-233-6 $14.95

Dark Angels
Lesbian Vampire Erotica
Edited by Pam Keesey

Dark Angels collects tales of lesbian vampires, the quintessential bad girls, archetypes of passion and terror. These tales of desire are so sharply erotic you'll swear you've been bitten!
ISBN 978-1-57344-252-7 $13.95

Ordering is easy! Call us toll free or fax us to place your MC/VISA order.
You can also mail the order form below with payment to:
Cleis Press, 2246 Sixth St., Berkeley, CA 94710.

ORDER FORM

QTY	TITLE	PRICE
_____	_____	_____
_____	_____	_____
_____	_____	_____
_____	_____	_____
_____	_____	_____
_____	_____	_____
_____	_____	_____

	SUBTOTAL	_____
	SHIPPING	_____
	SALES TAX	_____
	TOTAL	_____

Add $3.95 postage/handling for the first book ordered and $1.00 for each additional book. Outside North America, please contact us for shipping rates. California residents add 8.75% sales tax. Payment in U.S. dollars only.

★ **Free book of equal or lesser value. Shipping and applicable sales tax extra.**

Cleis Press • Phone: (800) 780-2279 • Fax: (510) 845-8001
orders@cleispress.com • www.cleispress.com
You'll find more great books on our website

Follow us on Twitter @cleispress • Friend/fan us on Facebook